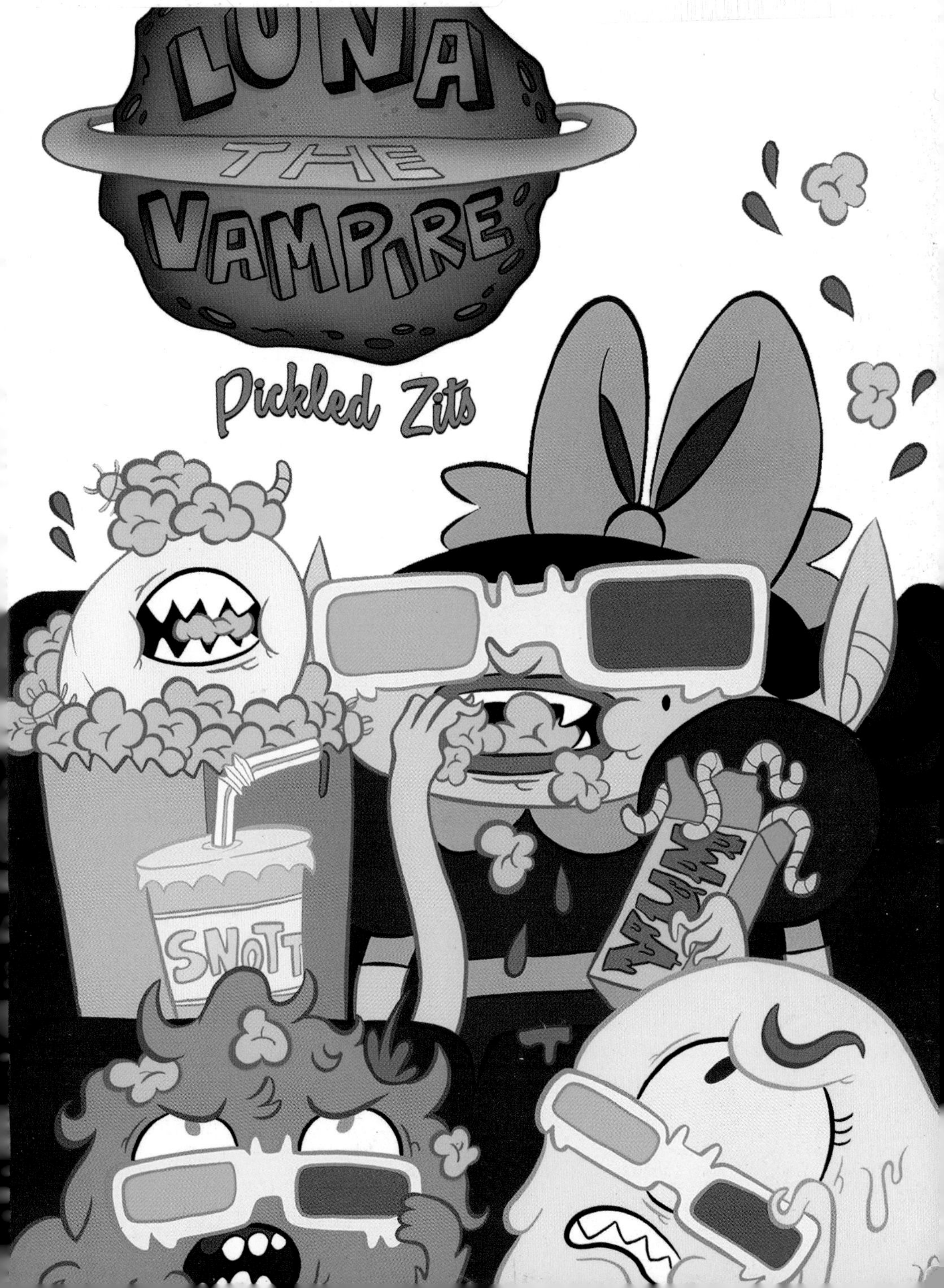
LUNA
THE
VAMPIRE
Pickled Zits
SNOTT
YUM

THE ADVENTURES OF
LUNA THE VAMPIRE
Pickled Zits

Become our fan on Facebook **facebook.com/idwpublishing**
Follow us on Twitter **@idwpublishing**
Subscribe to us on YouTube **youtube.com/idwpublishing**
See what's new on Tumblr **tumblr.idwpublishing.com**
Check us out on Instagram **instagram.com/idwpublishing**

IDW
www.IDWPUBLISHING.com

Greg Goldstein, President & Publisher
Robbie Robbins, EVP & Sr. Art Director
Matthew Ruzicka, CPA, Chief Financial Officer
David Hedgecock, Associate Publisher
Laurie Windrow, Senior Vice President of Sales & Marketing
Lorelei Bunjes, VP of Digital Services
Eric Moss, Sr. Director, Licensing & Business Development

Ted Adams, Founder & CEO of IDW Media Holdings

ISBN: 978-1-68405-260-8   21 20 19 18   1 2 3 4

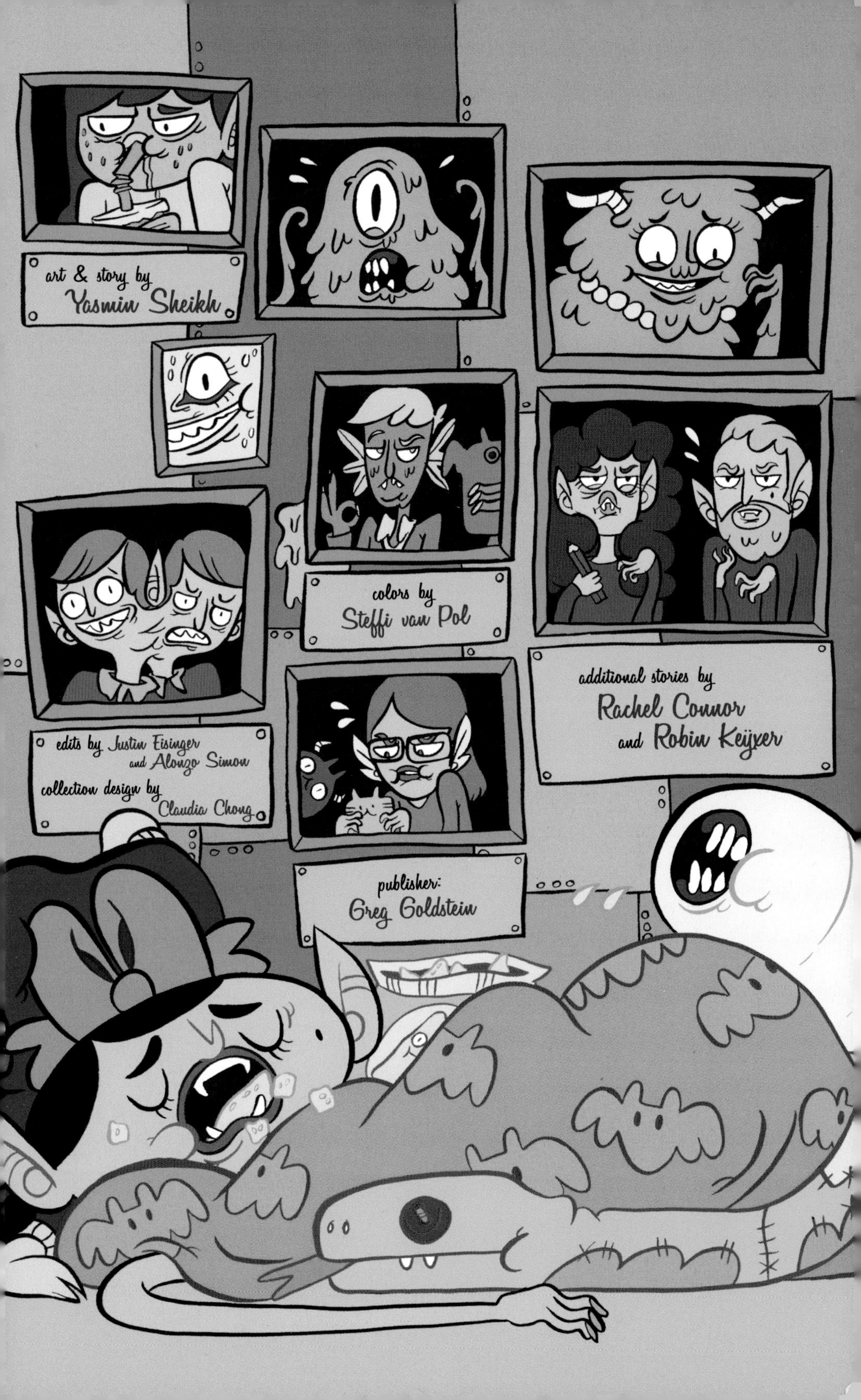

art & story by
Yasmin Sheikh
colors by
Steffi van Pol
additional stories by
Rachel Connor
and Robin Keijxer
edits by Justin Eisinger
and Alonzo Simon
collection design by
Claudia Chong
publisher:
Greg Goldstein

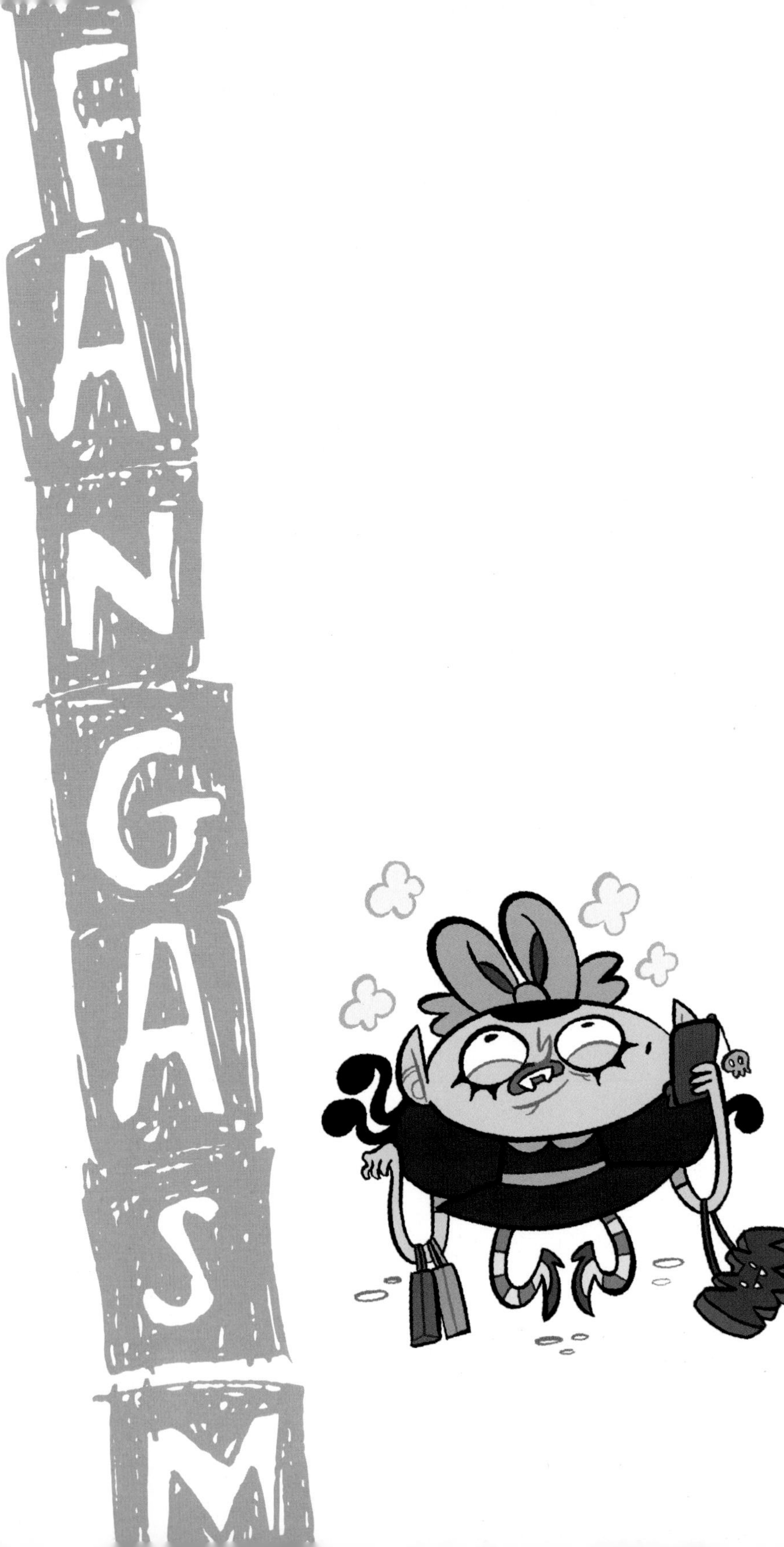
FANGASM

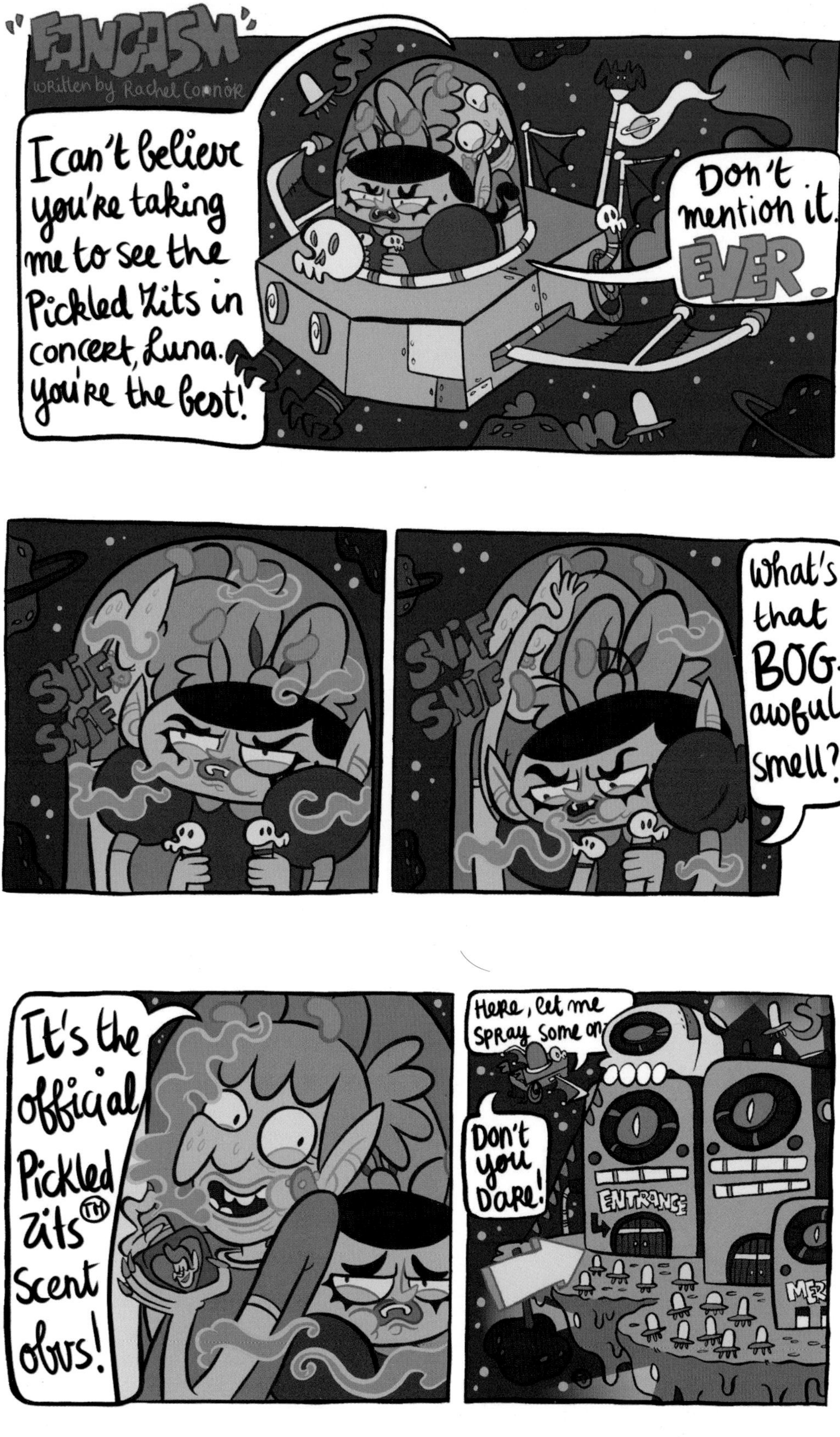
"FANGASM"
written by Rachel Connor
I can't believe you're taking me to see the Pickled Zits in concert, Luna. You're the best!
Don't mention it. EVER.
SNIF SNIF
SNIF SNIF
What's that BOG-awful smell?!
It's the official Pickled Zits™ scent obvs!
Here, let me spray some on.
Don't you dare!
ENTRANCE
MER

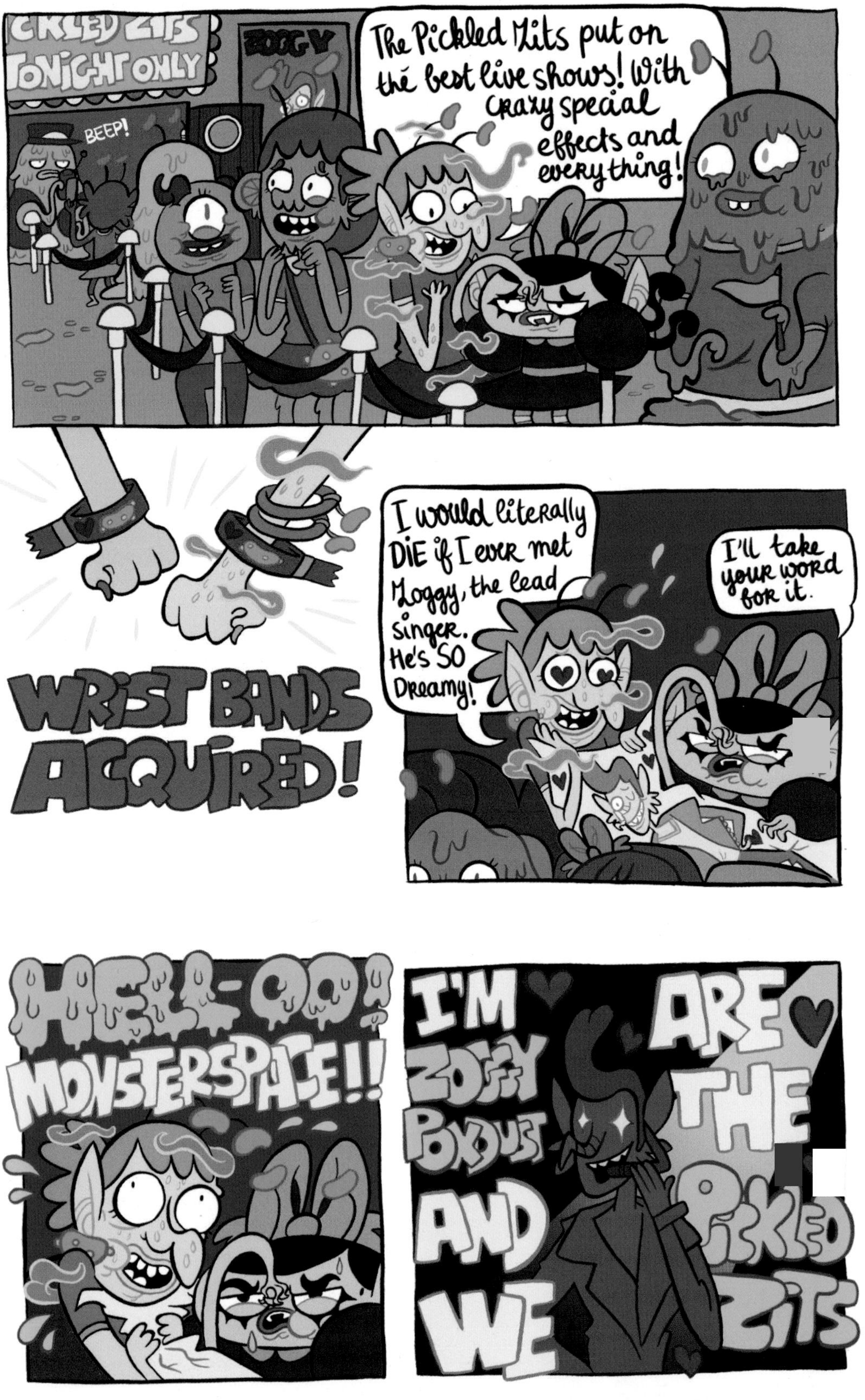
CKLED ZITS
TONIGHT ONLY
ZOGGY
BEEP!
The Pickled Zits put on the best live shows! With crazy special effects and everything!
WRIST BANDS ACQUIRED!
I would literally DIE if I ever met Zoggy, the lead singer. He's SO Dreamy!
I'll take your word for it.
HELL-OO MONSTERSPACE!!
I'M ZOGGY POXDUST AND WE ARE THE PICKLED ZITS

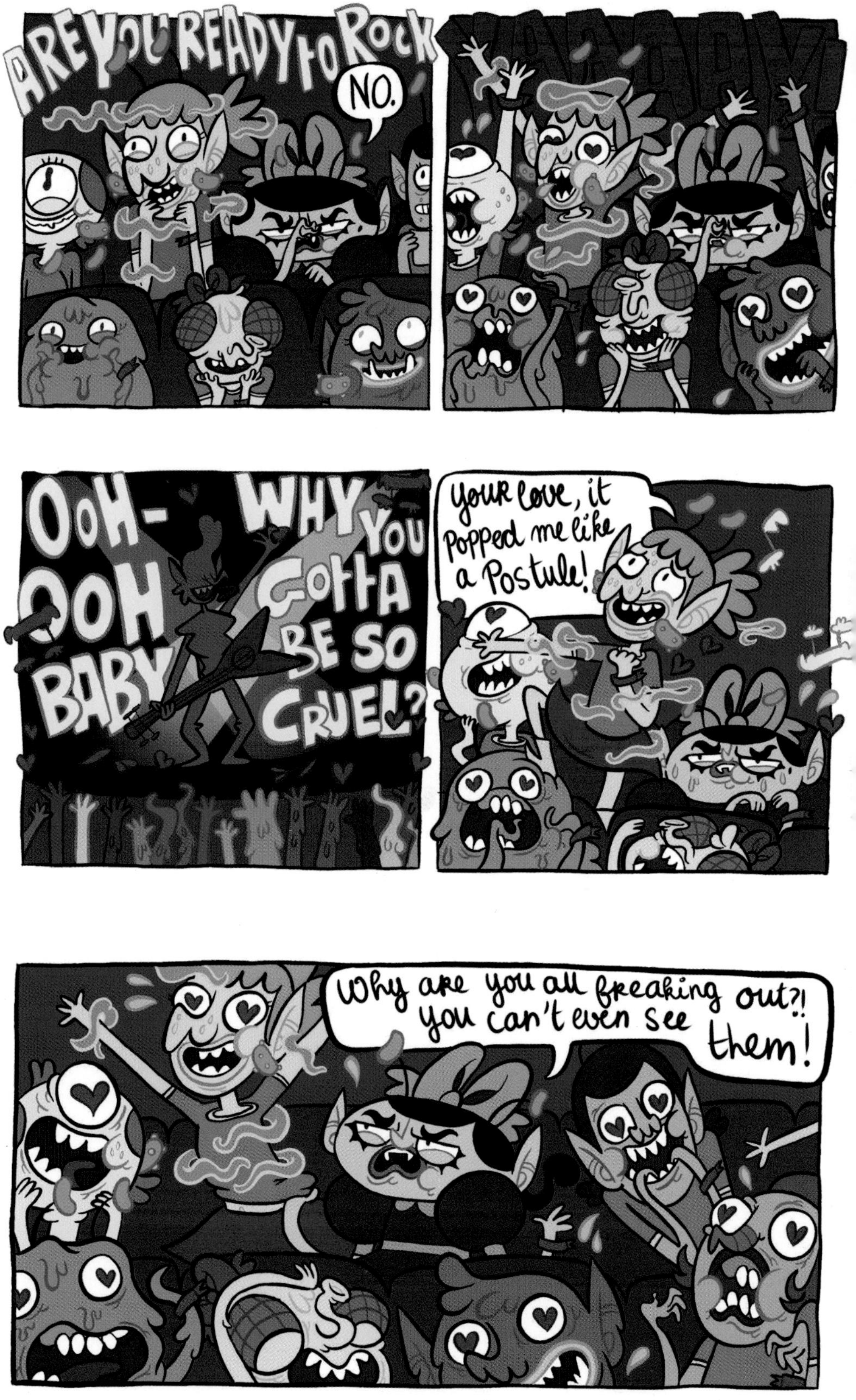

ARE YOU READY TO ROCK
NO.
YAAAAY!
OOH-OOH BABY
WHY YOU GOTTA BE SO CRUEL?
Your love, it popped me like a postule!
Why are you all freaking out?! You can't even see them!

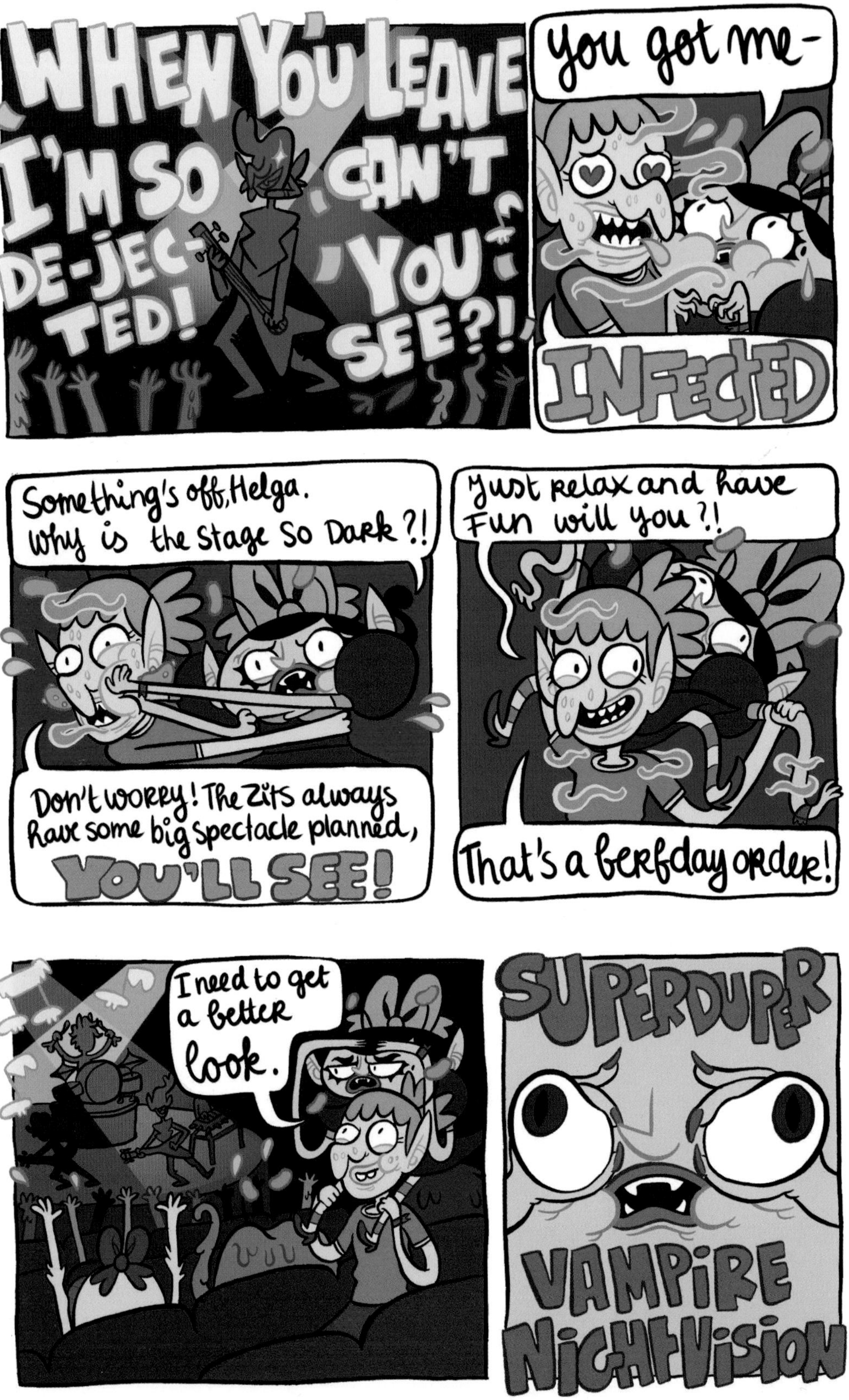
WHEN YOU LEAVE I'M SO DE-JEC-TED! CAN'T YOU SEE?!
You got me-
INFECTED
Something's off, Helga. Why is the Stage So Dark?!
Don't worry! The Zits always have some big spectacle planned,
YOU'LL SEE!
Just relax and have Fun will you?!
That's a berfday order!
I need to get a better look.
SUPERDUPER
VAMPIRE NIGHTVISION

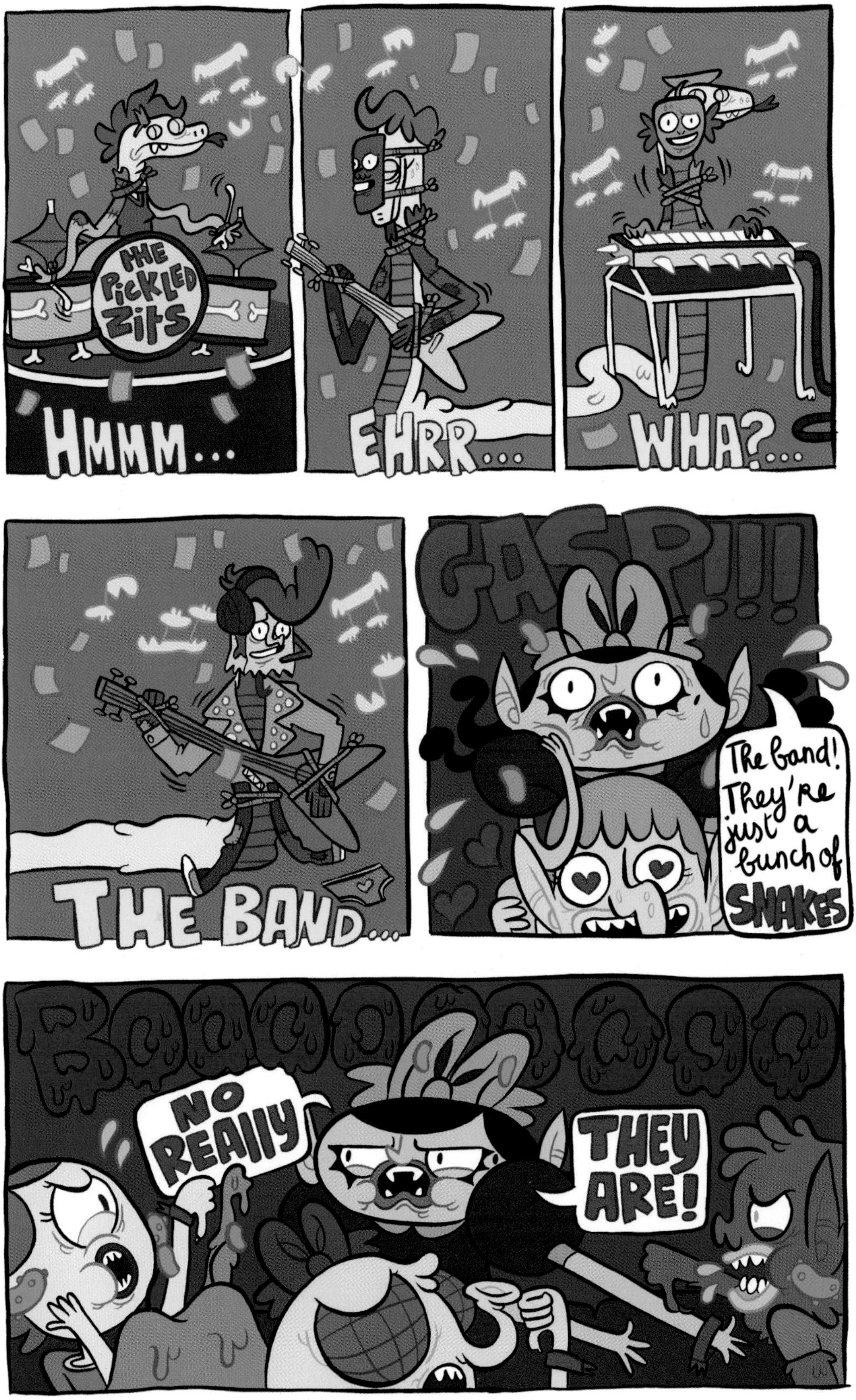
THE PICKLED ZITS
HMMM...
EHRR...
WHA?...
THE BAND...
GASP!!!
The band! They're just a bunch of SNAKES
BOOOOOOOOOO
NO REALLY
THEY ARE!

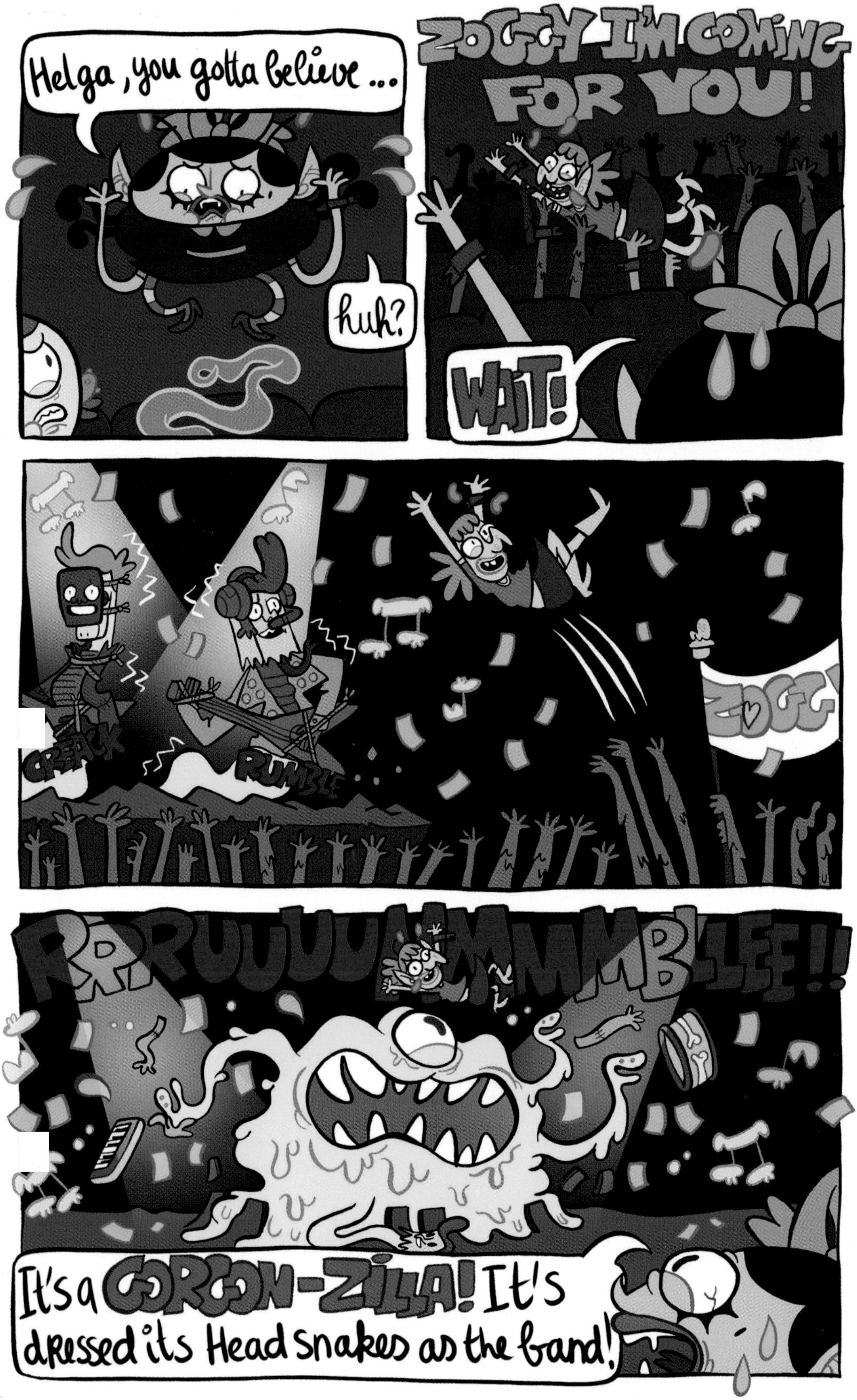
Helga, you gotta believe...
huh?
ZOGGY I'M COMING FOR YOU!
WAIT!
CREACK
RUMBLE
ZOGGY
RRRUUUUMMMMBLLEE!!
It's a GORGON-ZILLA! It's dressed its Head snakes as the band!

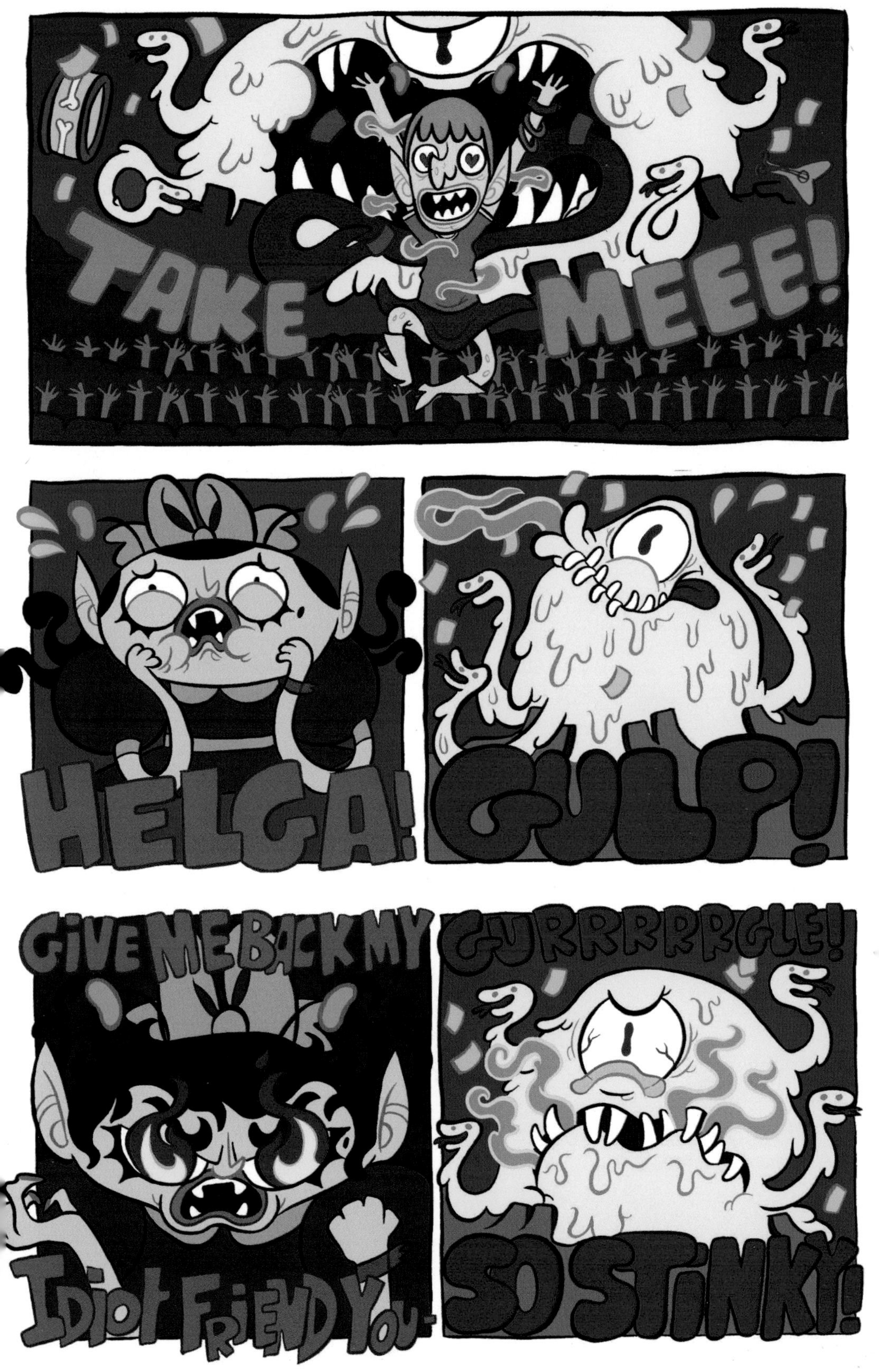
TAKE MEEE!
HELGA!
GULP!
GIVE ME BACK MY
IDIOT FRIEND YOU-
GURRRRRGLE!
SO STINKY!

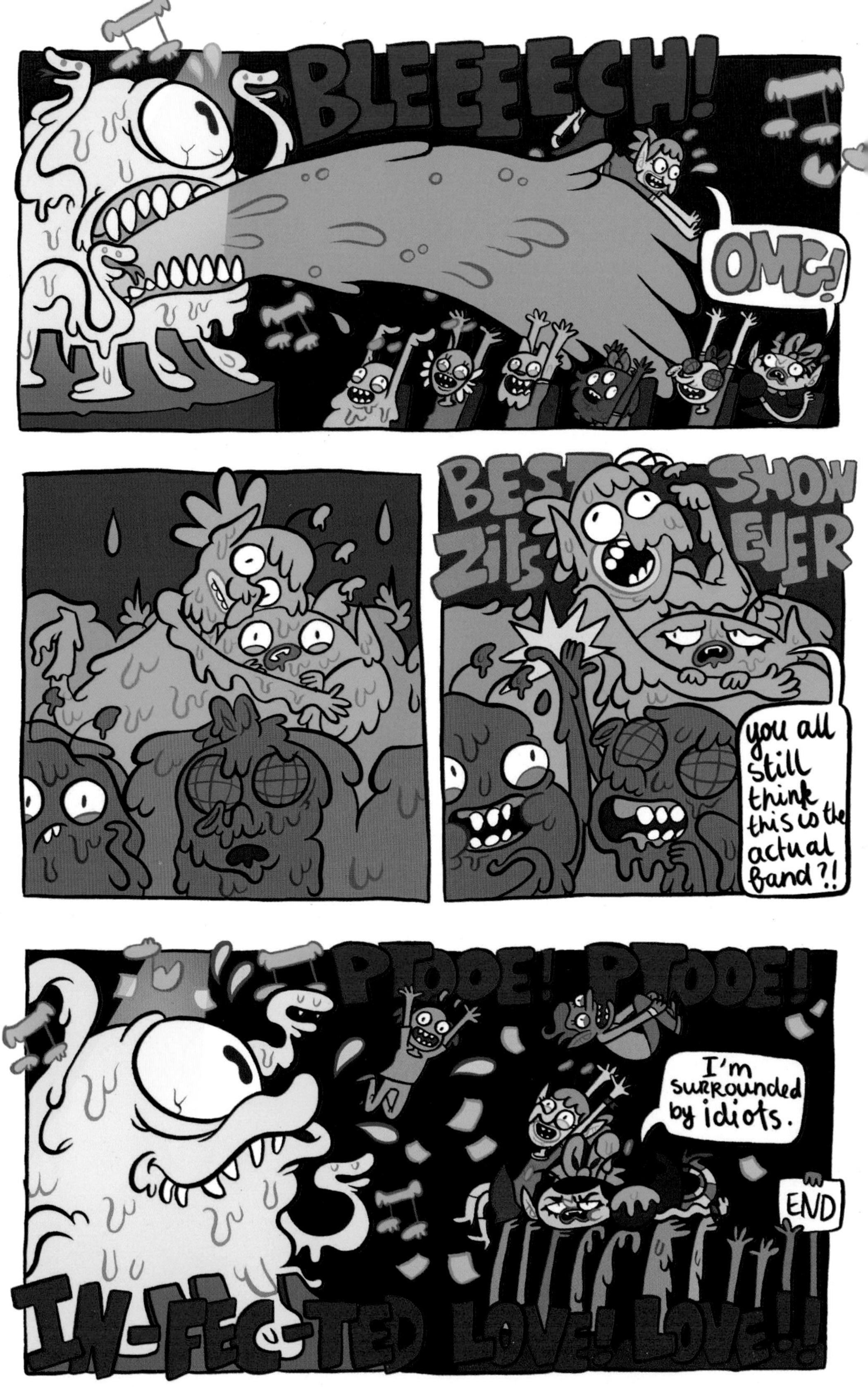
BLEEEECH!
OMG!
BEST SHOW EVER
Zits
you all still think this is the actual band?!
PTOOE! PTOOE!
I'm surrounded by idiots.
END
IN-FEC-TED LOVE! LOVE!!

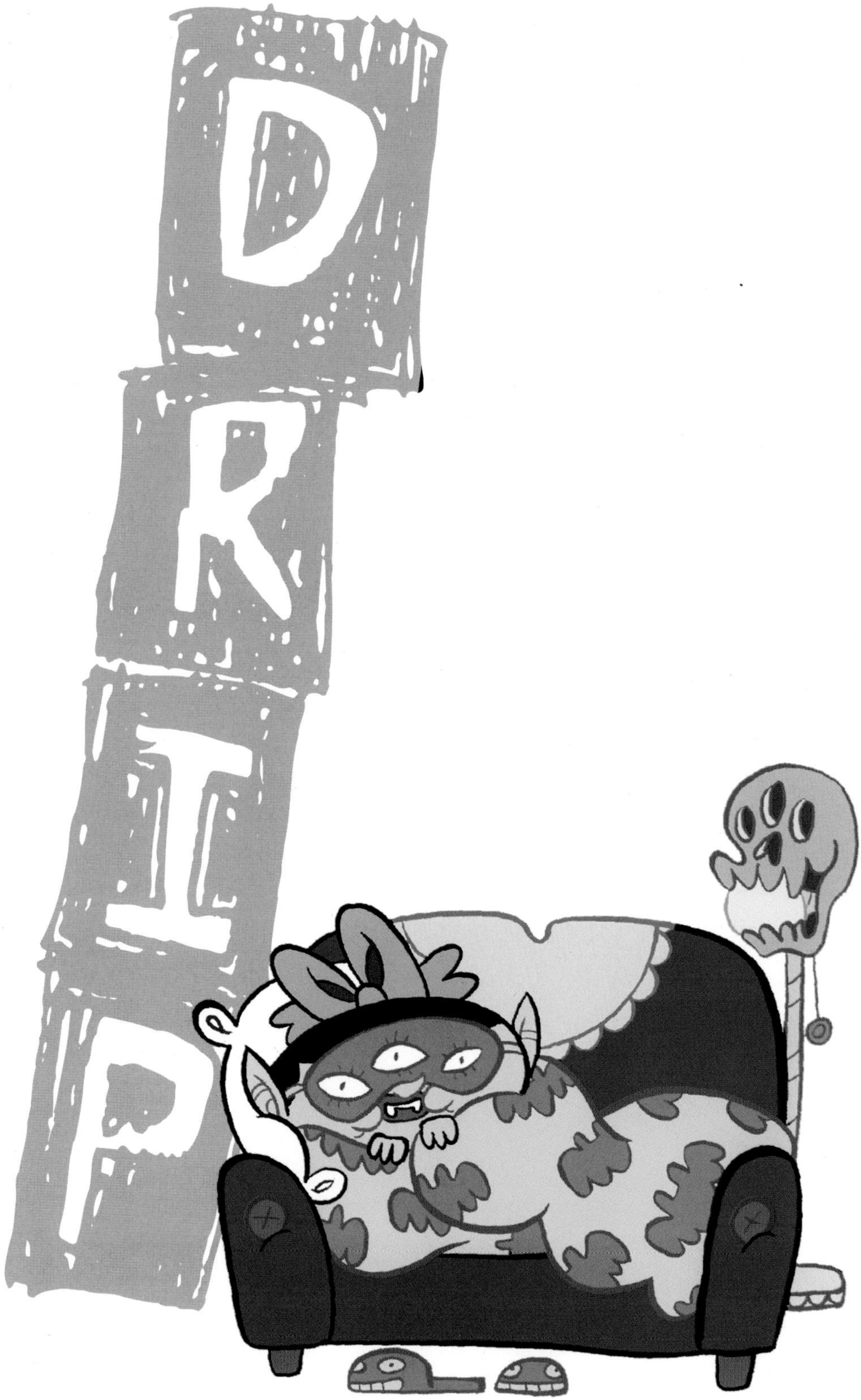
DRIP

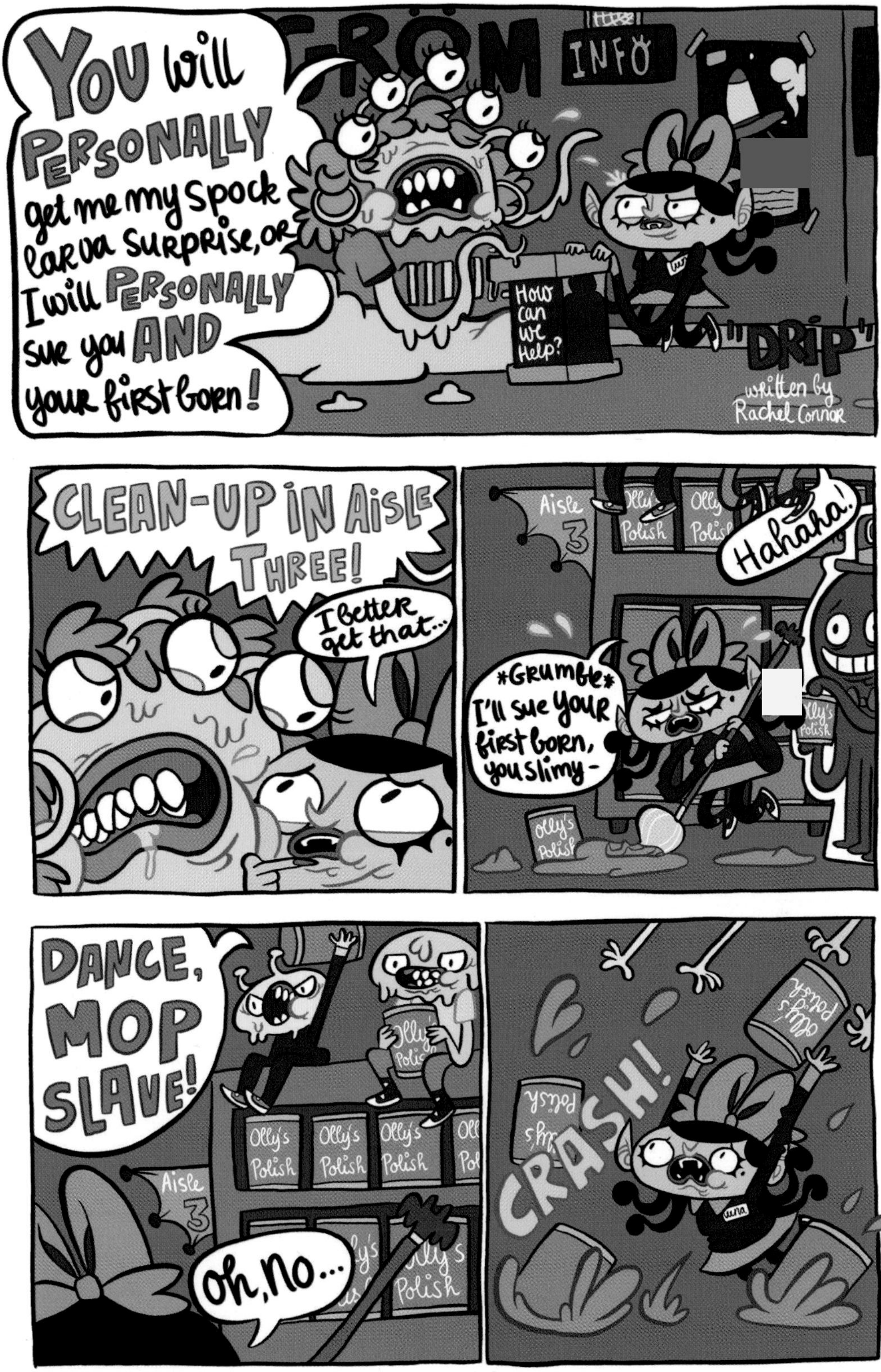
YOU will PERSONALLY get me my Spock larva surprise, or I will PERSONALLY sue you AND your first born!
GRÖM
INFO
How can we Help?
"DRIP"
written by Rachel Connor
CLEAN-UP IN AISLE THREE!
I better get that...
Aisle 3
Olly's Polish
Hahaha!
Grumble I'll sue your first born, you slimy-
Olly's Polish
DANCE, MOP SLAVE!
Olly's Polish
Aisle 3
Oh, no...
CRASH!
Olly's Polish

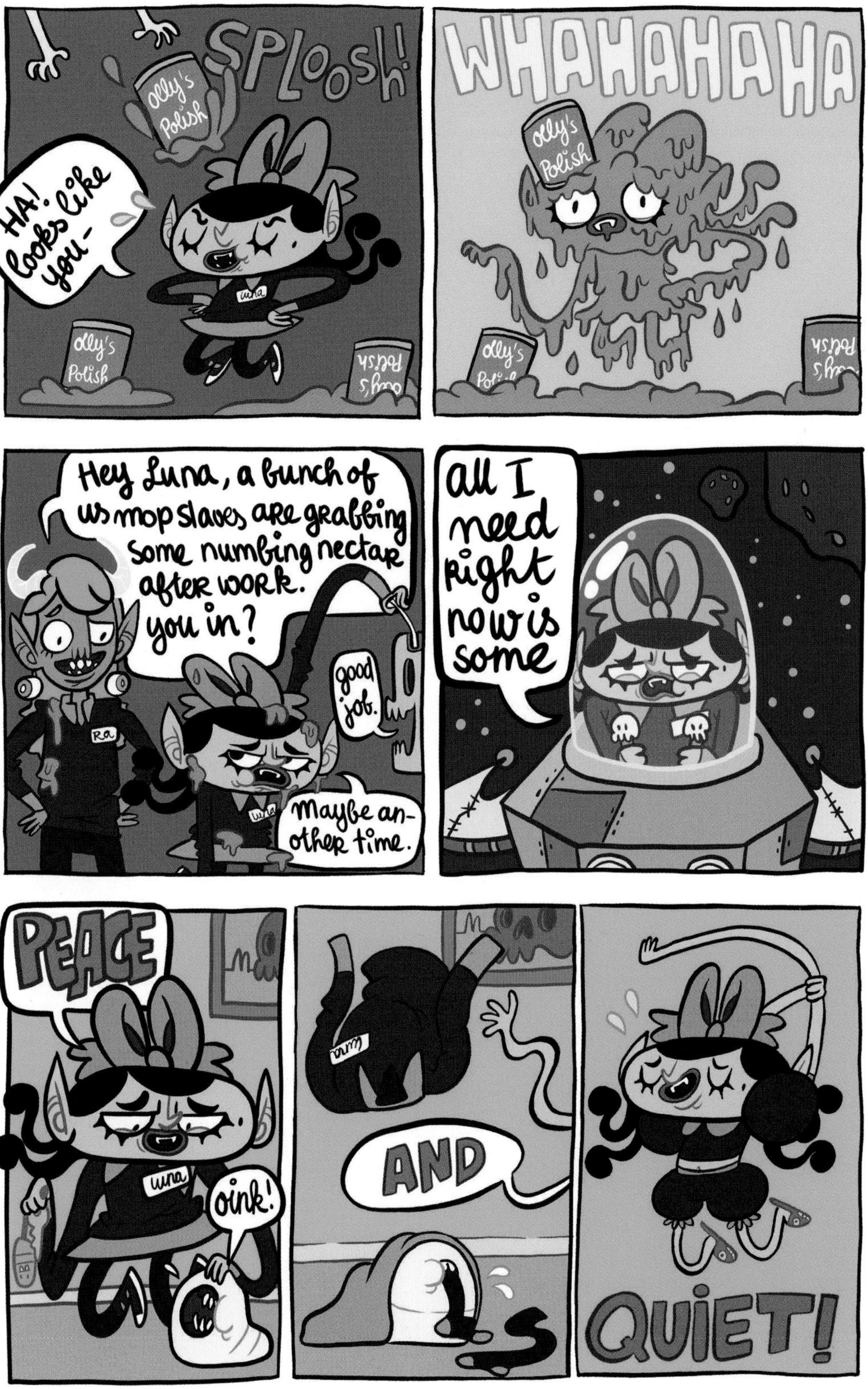
SPLOOSH!
olly's Polish
HA! looks like you-
luna
olly's Polish
WHAHAHAHAHA
olly's Polish
Hey Luna, a bunch of us mop slaves are grabbing some numbing nectar after work. you in?
Ra
good job.
Maybe an-other time.
all I need right now is some
PEACE
luna
oink!
AND
QUIET!

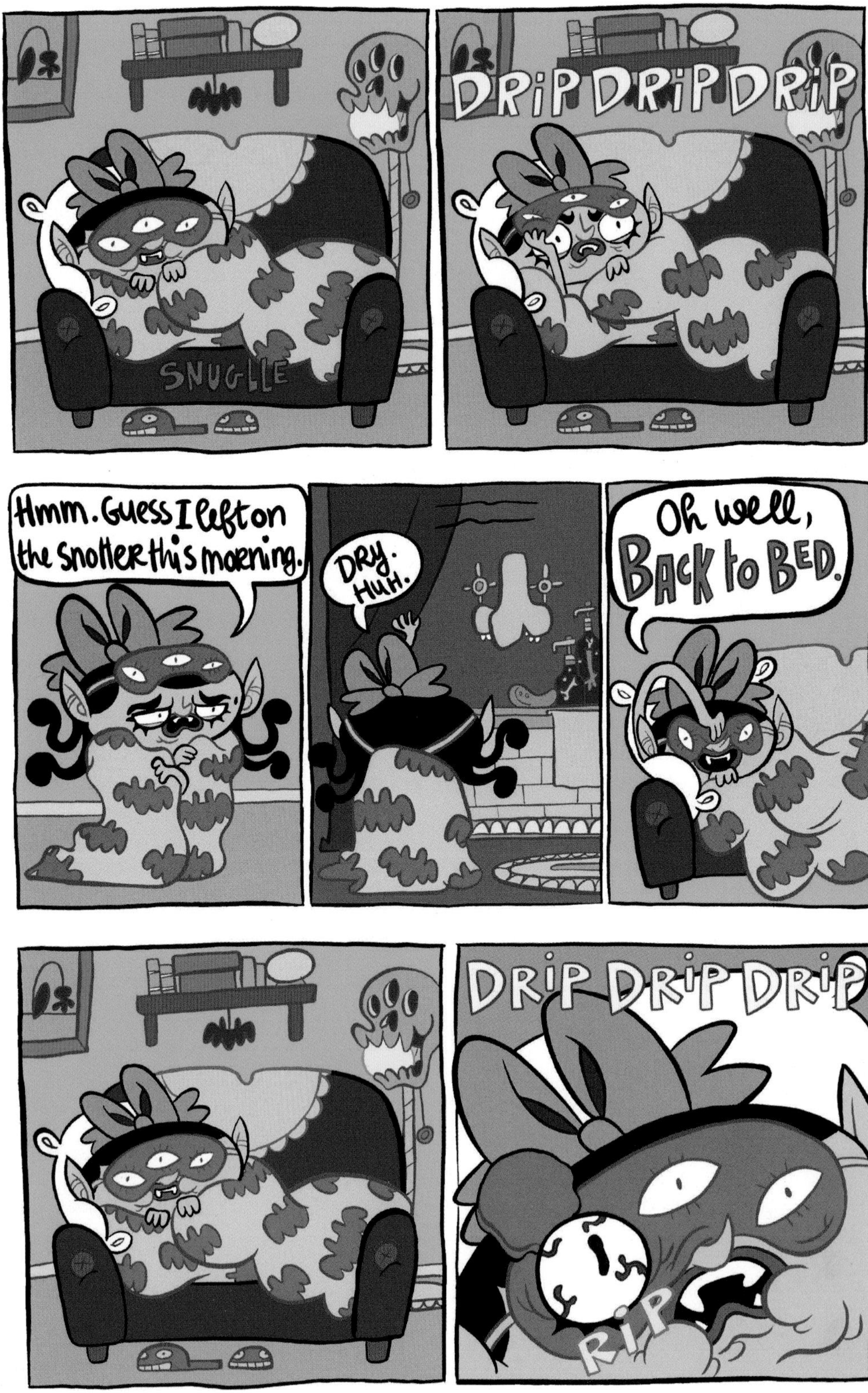
SNUGGLE
DRIP DRIP DRIP
Hmm. Guess I left on the snotter this morning.
DRY. HUH.
Oh well, BACK to BED.
DRIP DRIP DRIP
RIP

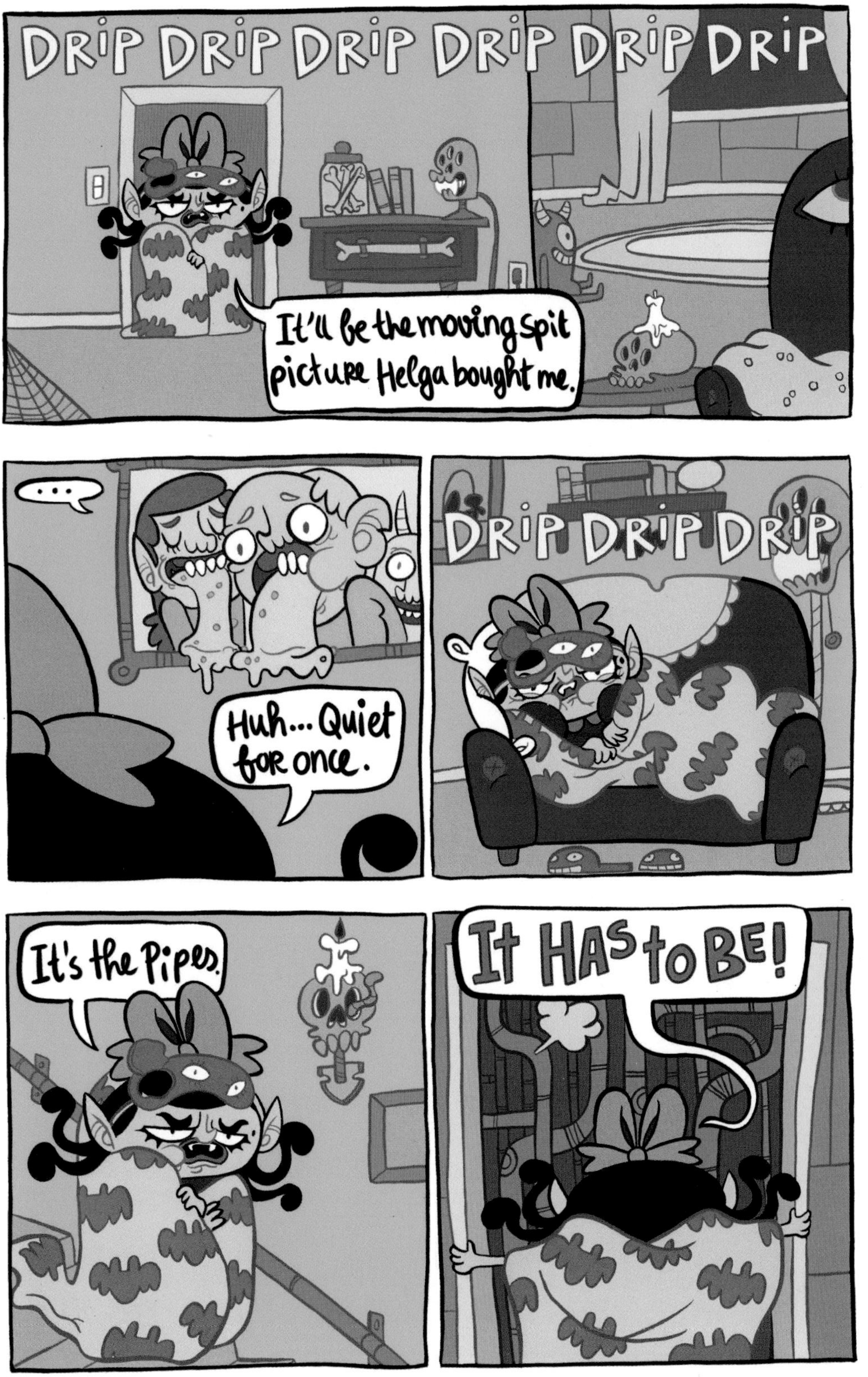
DRIP DRIP DRIP DRIP DRIP DRIP
It'll be the moving spit picture Helga bought me.
...
Huh... Quiet for once.
DRIP DRIP DRIP
It's the Pipes.
It HAS to BE!

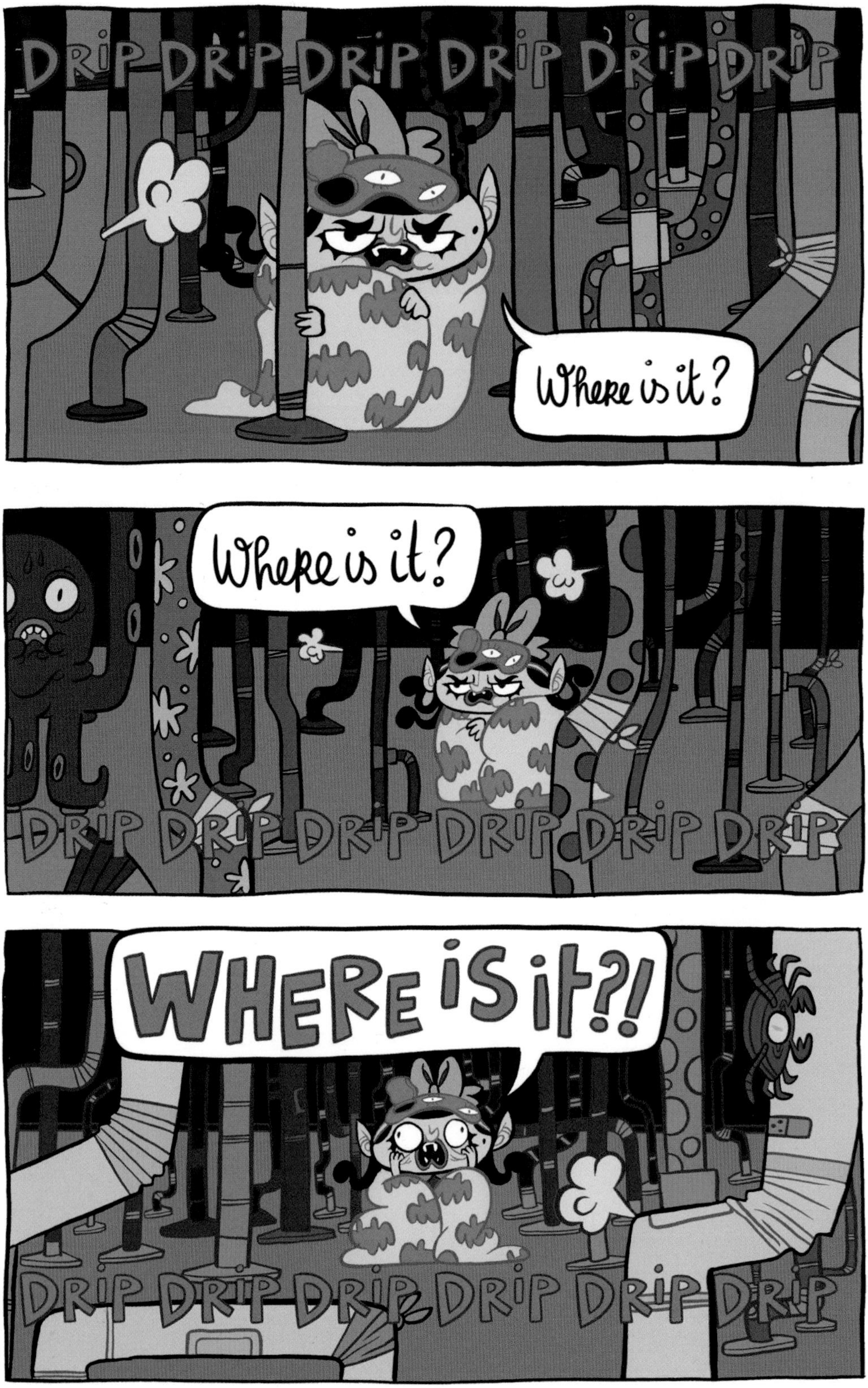
DRIP DRIP DRIP DRIP DRIP DRIP
Where is it?
Where is it?
DRIP DRIP DRIP DRIP DRIP DRIP
WHERE IS IT?!
DRIP DRIP DRIP DRIP DRIP DRIP

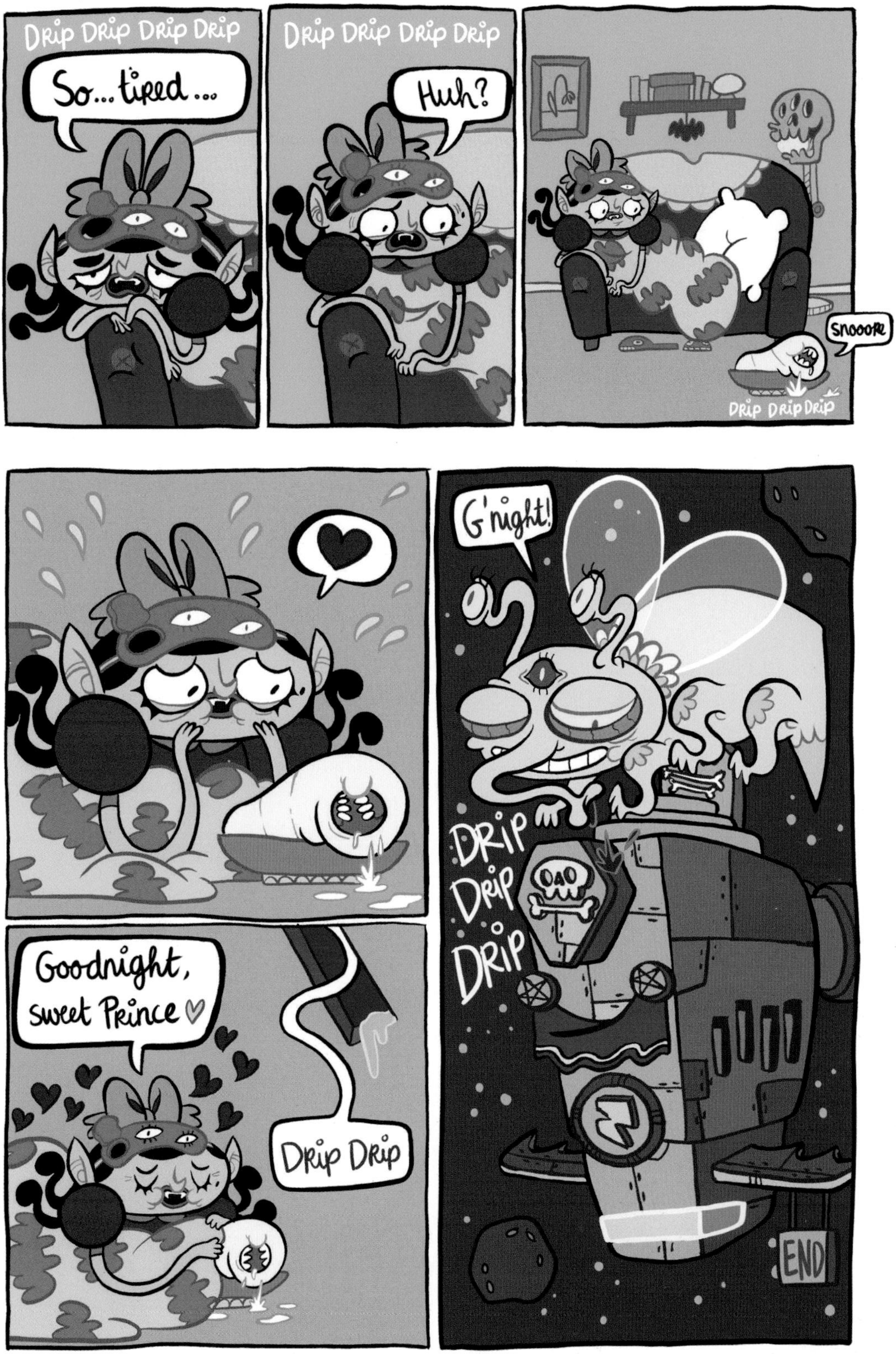
DRIP DRIP DRIP DRIP
So... tired...
DRIP DRIP DRIP DRIP
Huh?
SNOOORE
DRIP DRIP DRIP
G'night!
DRIP
DRIP
DRIP
Goodnight, sweet Prince
DRIP DRIP
END

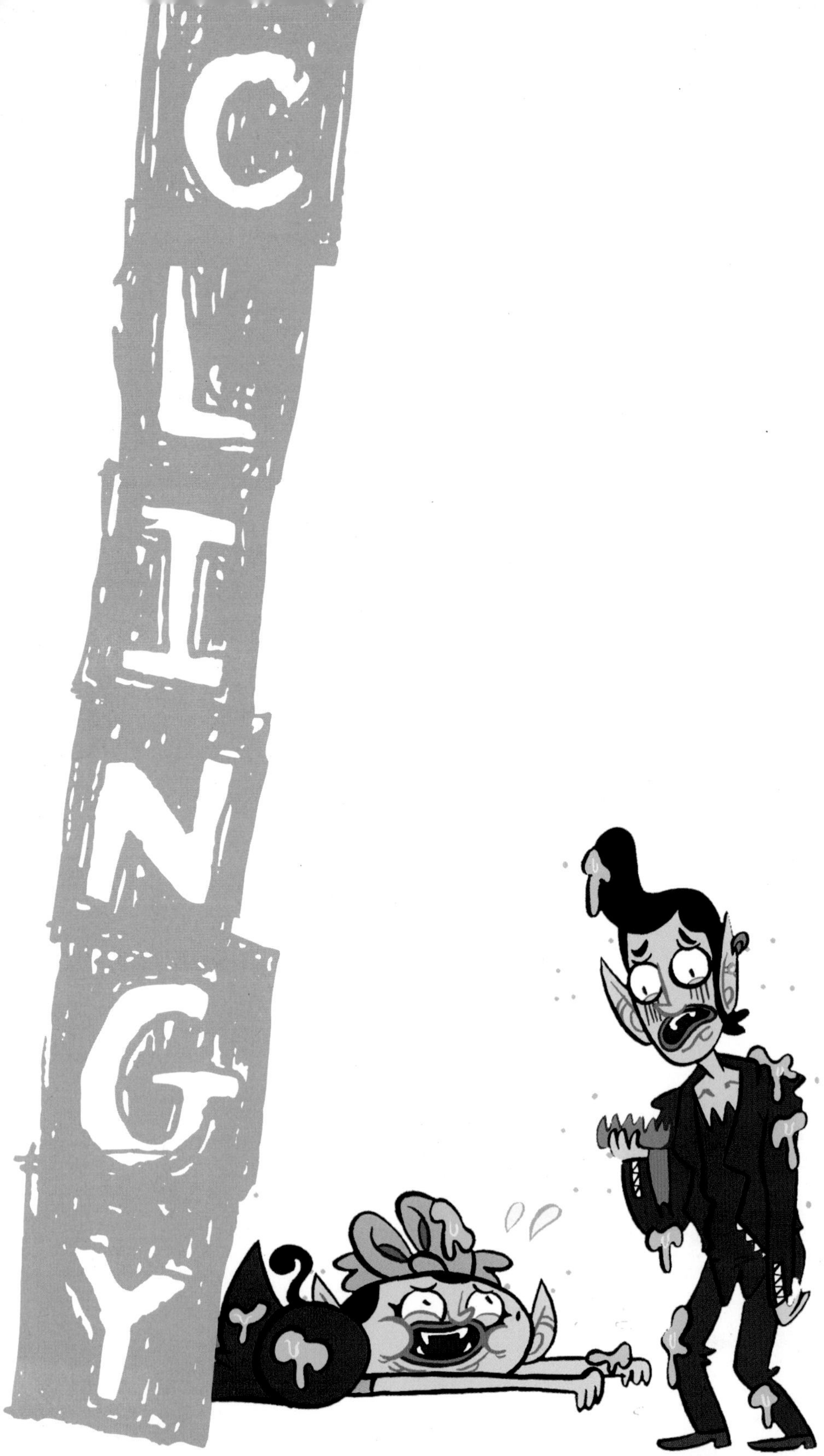
CLINGY

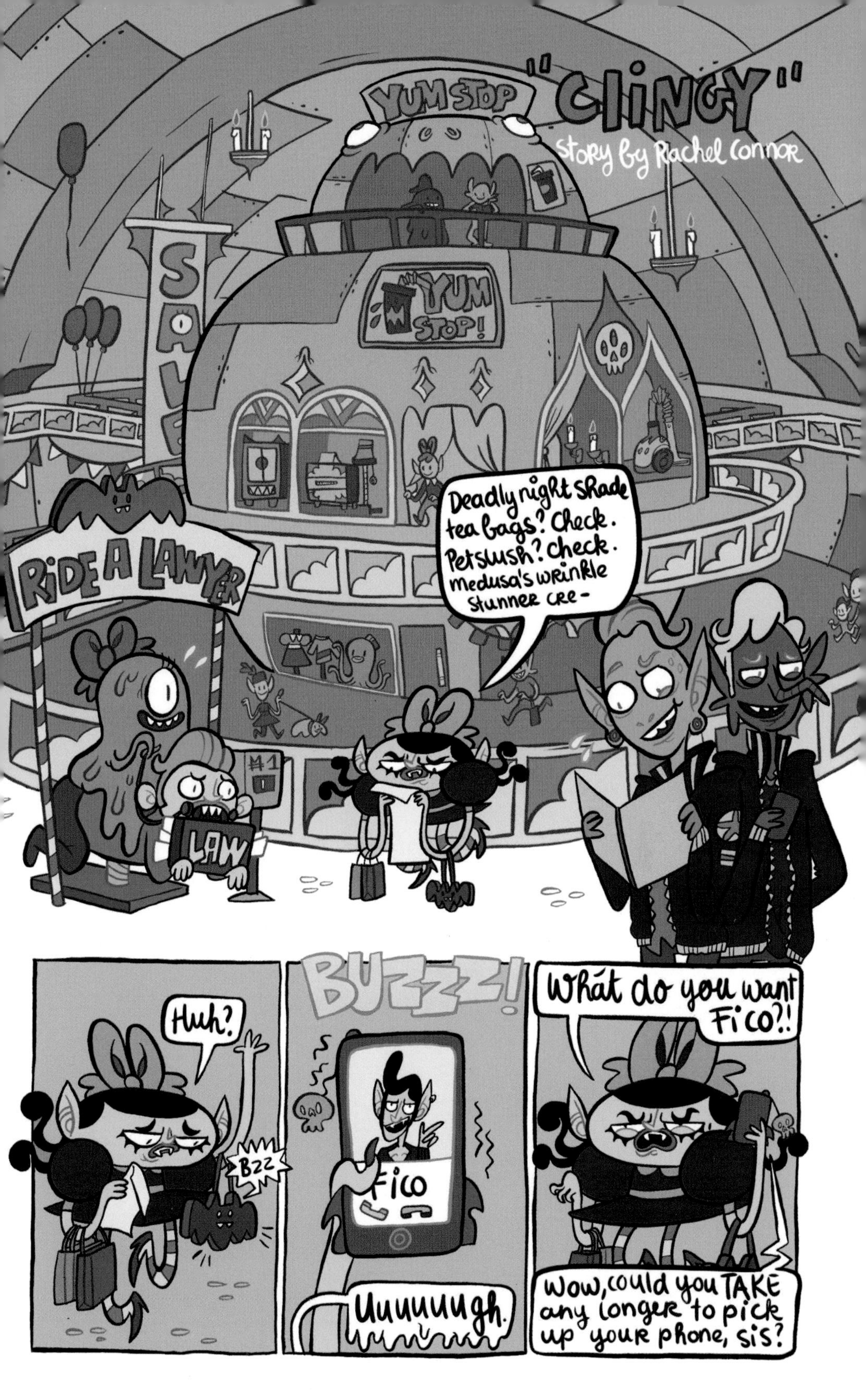
"CLINGY"
Story by Rachel Connor
YUM STOP
YUM STOP!
SALE
RIDE A LAWYER
LAW
Deadly night shade tea bags? Check. Petslush? Check. medusa's wrinkle stunner cre-
Huh?
BZZ
BUZZZ!
Fico
Uuuuuugh.
What do you want Fico?!
Wow, could you TAKE any longer to pick up your phone, sis?

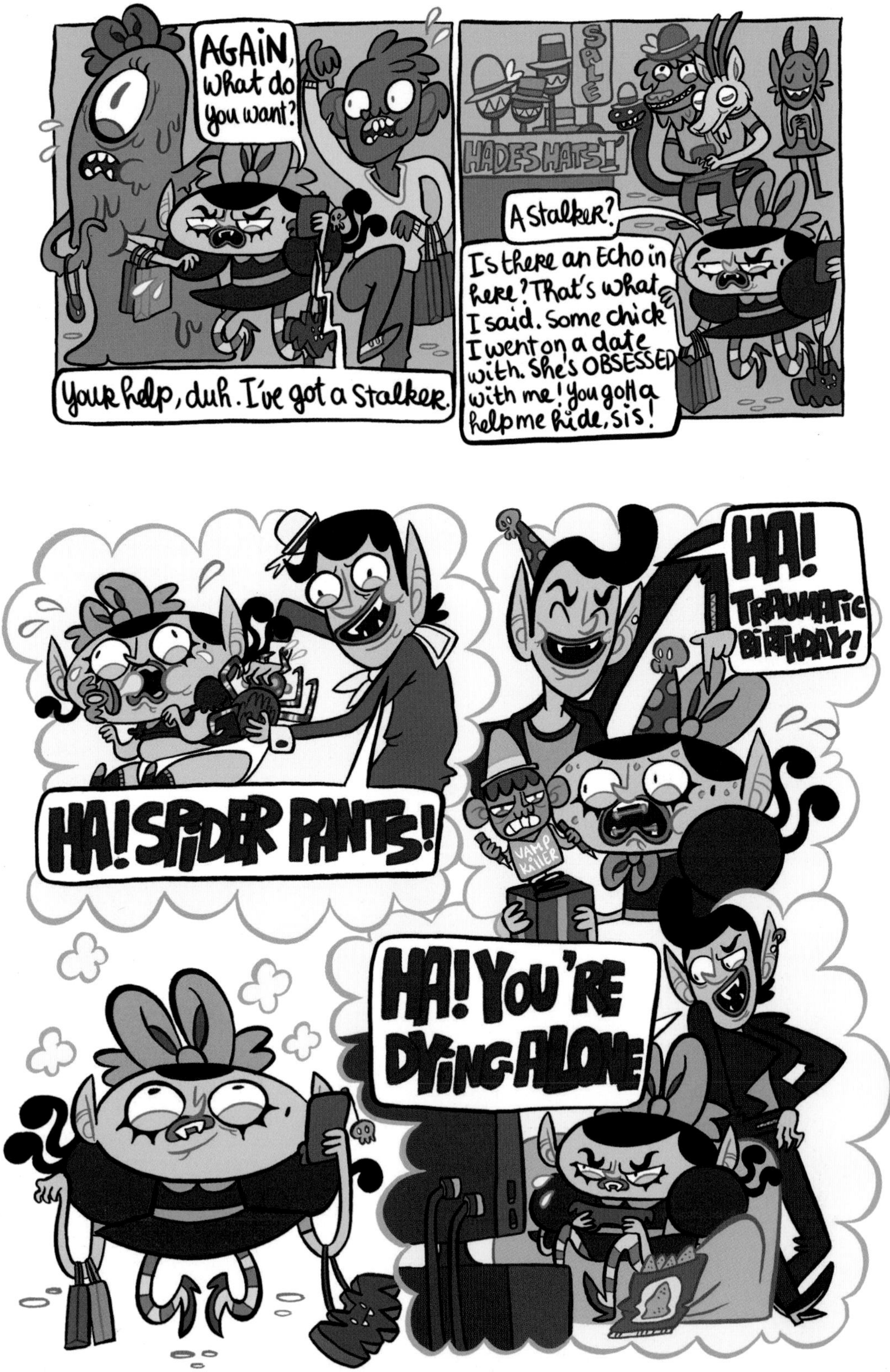
AGAIN, what do you want?
Your help, duh. I've got a stalker.
SALE
HADES HATS!
A Stalker?
Is there an Echo in here? That's what I said. Some chick I went on a date with. She's OBSESSED with me! You gotta help me hide, sis!
HA! SPIDER PANTS!
HA! TRAUMATIC BIRTHDAY!
VAMP KILLER
HA! YOU'RE DYING ALONE

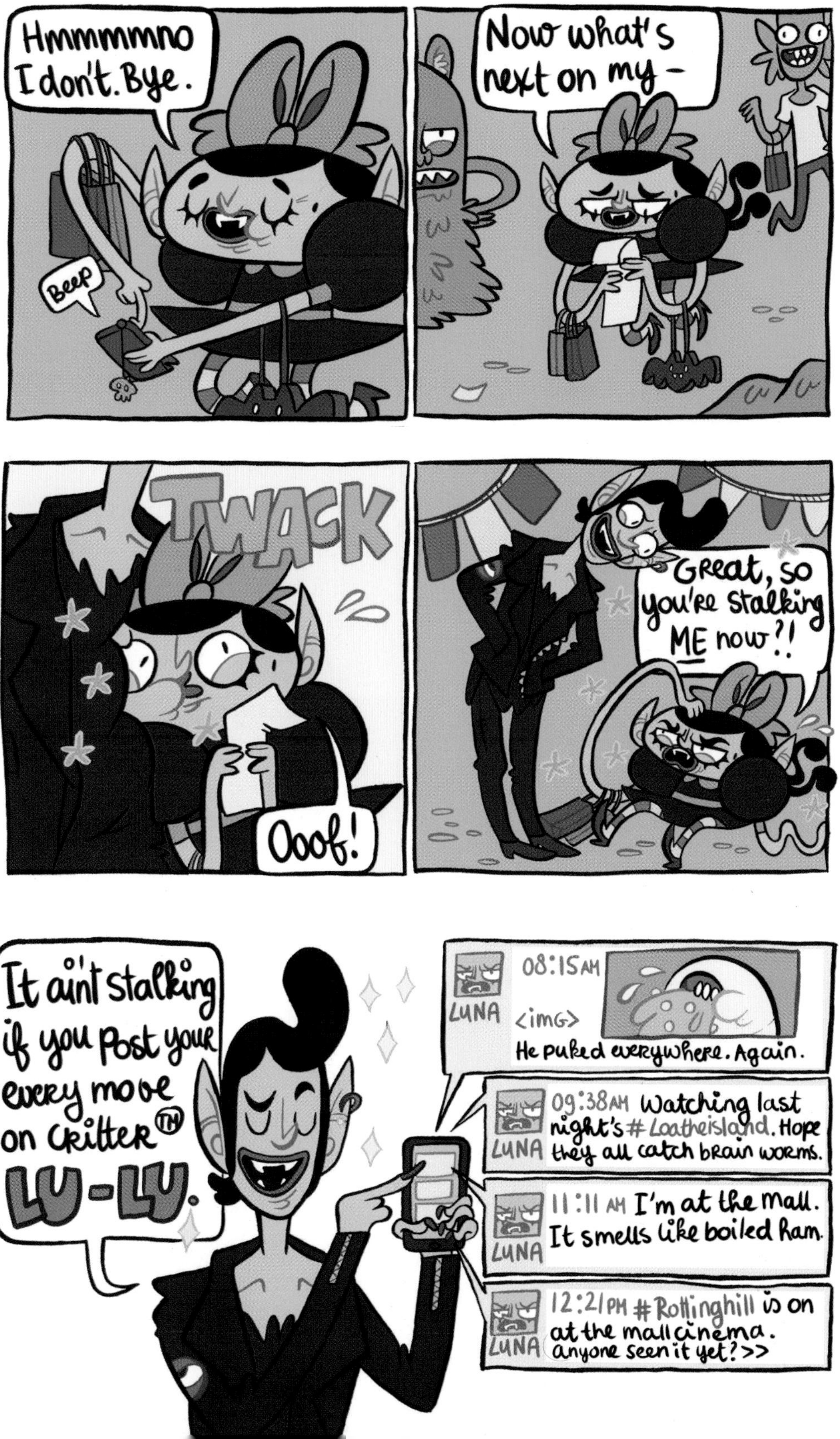
Hmmmmno I don't. Bye.
Beep
Now what's next on my-
TWACK
Ooof!
Great, so you're stalking ME now?!
It ain't stalking if you post your every move on Critter™ LU-LU.
LUNA 08:15AM <imG> He puked everywhere. Again.
LUNA 09:38AM Watching last night's #Loatheisland. Hope they all catch brain worms.
LUNA 11:11 AM I'm at the mall. It smells like boiled ham.
LUNA 12:21PM #Rollinghill is on at the mall cinema. anyone seen it yet?>>

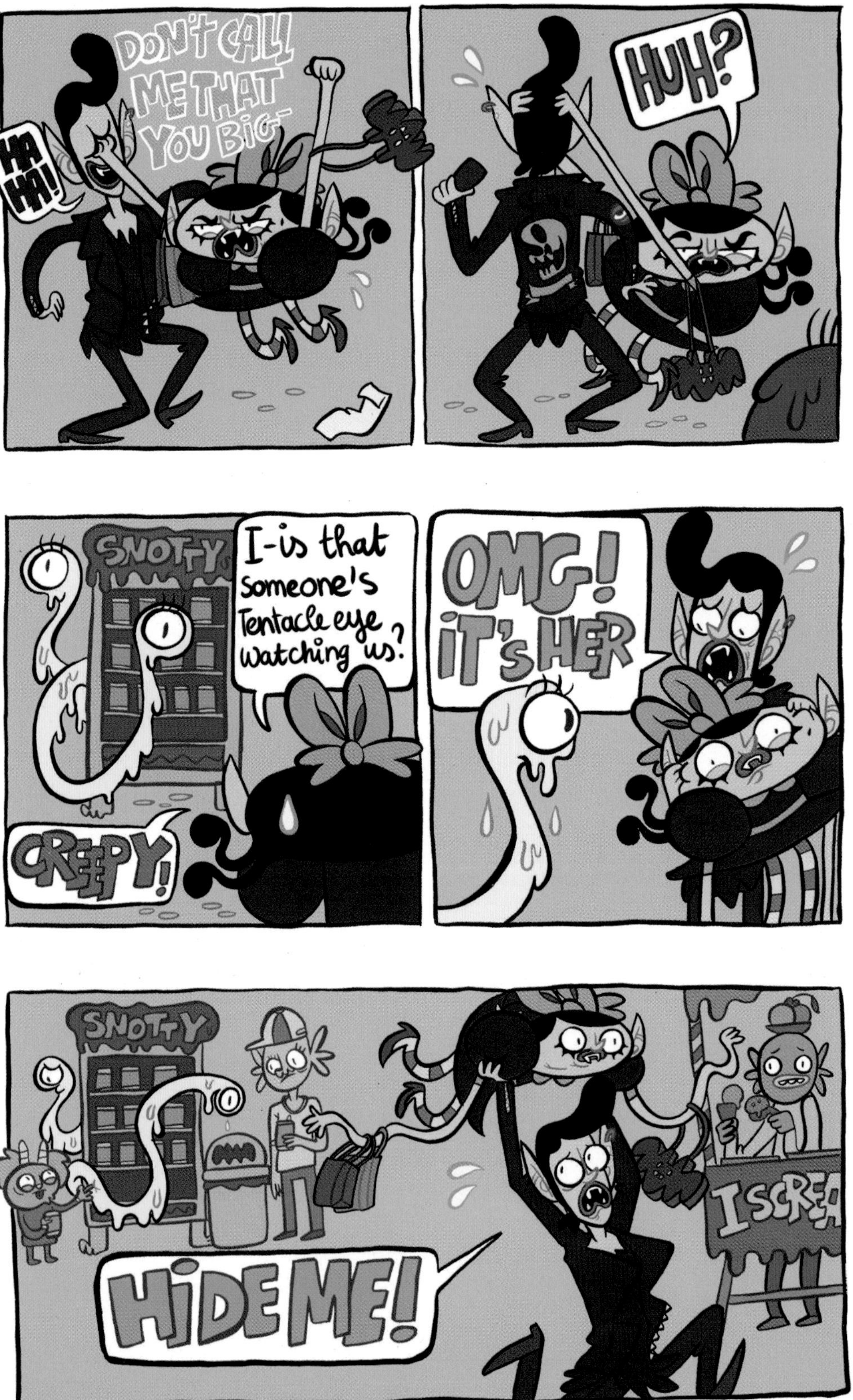
DON'T CALL ME THAT YOU BIG-
HA HA!
HUH?
I-is that someone's Tentacle eye watching us?
SNOTTY
CREEPY!
OMG! IT'S HER
SNOTTY
ISCREA
HIDE ME!

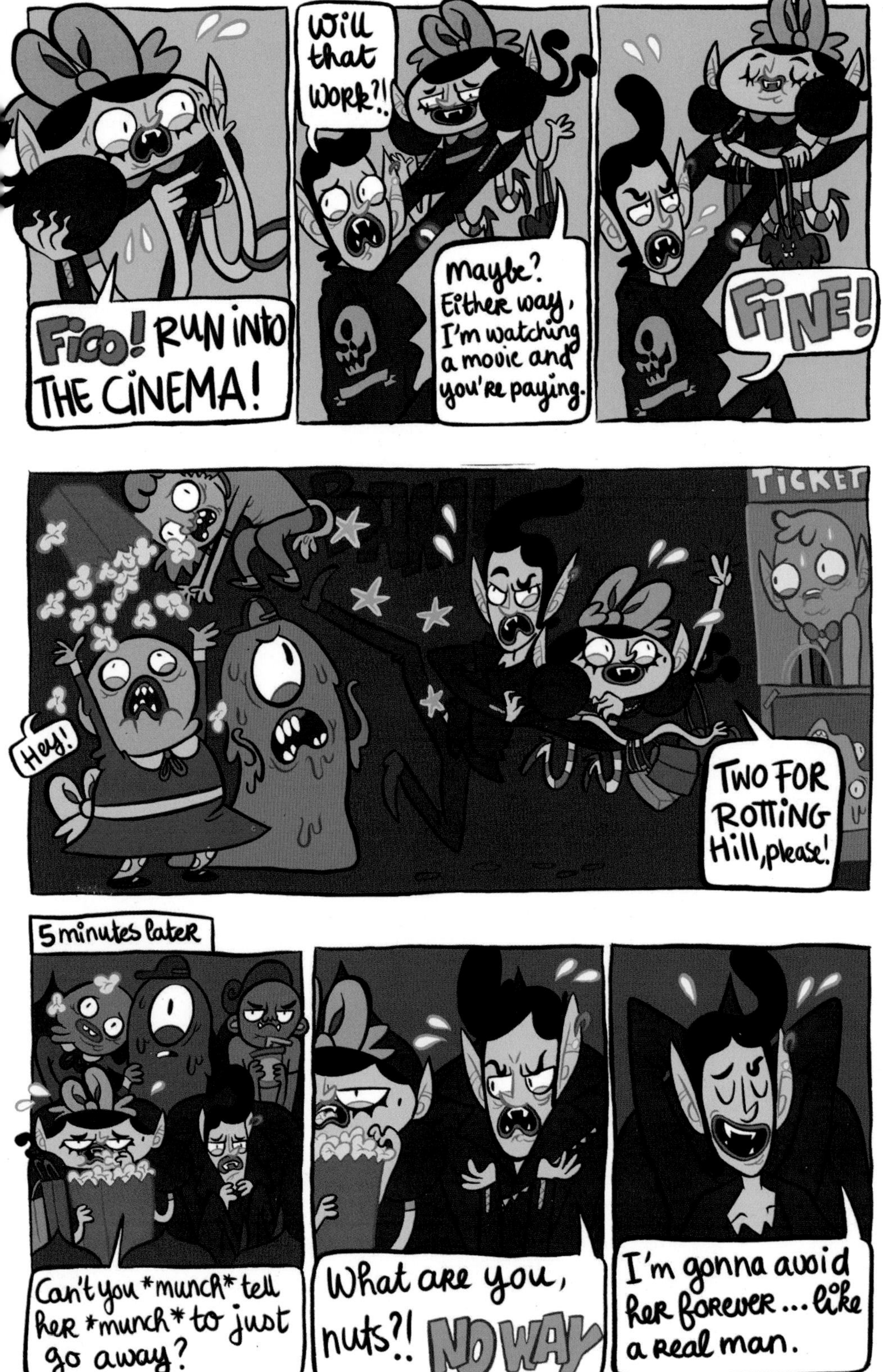
FICO! RUN INTO THE CINEMA!
Will that work?!
Maybe? Either way, I'm watching a movie and you're paying.
FINE!
TICKET
Hey!
TWO FOR ROTTING Hill, please!
5 minutes later
Can't you *munch* tell her *munch* to just go away?
What are you, nuts?!
NO WAY
I'm gonna avoid her forever... like a real man.

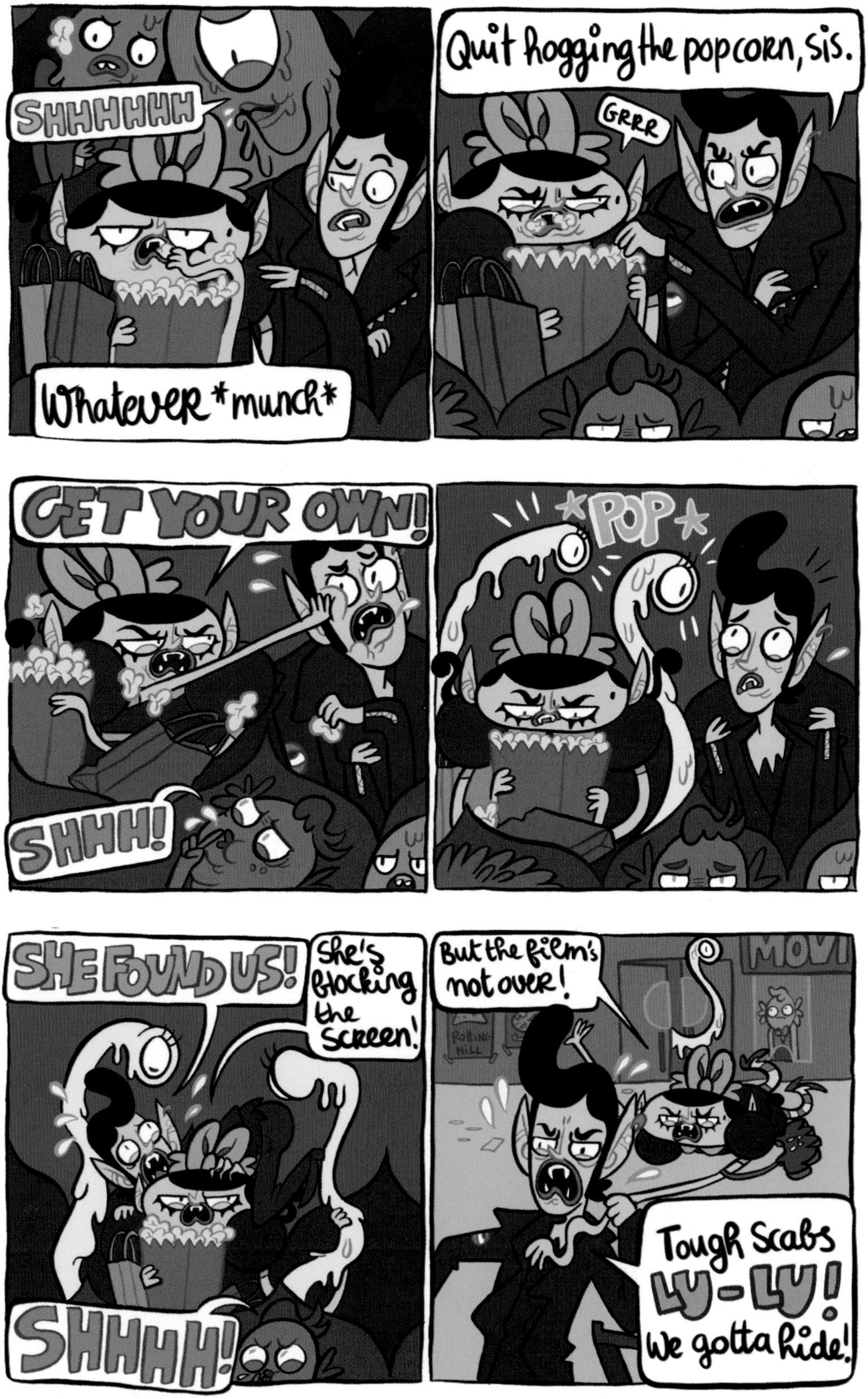
SHHHHHH
Whatever *munch*
Quit hogging the popcorn, sis.
GRRR
GET YOUR OWN!
SHHH!
POP
SHE FOUND US!
She's blocking the screen!
SHHHH!
But the film's not over!
MOVI
Tough Scabs LU-LU! We gotta hide!

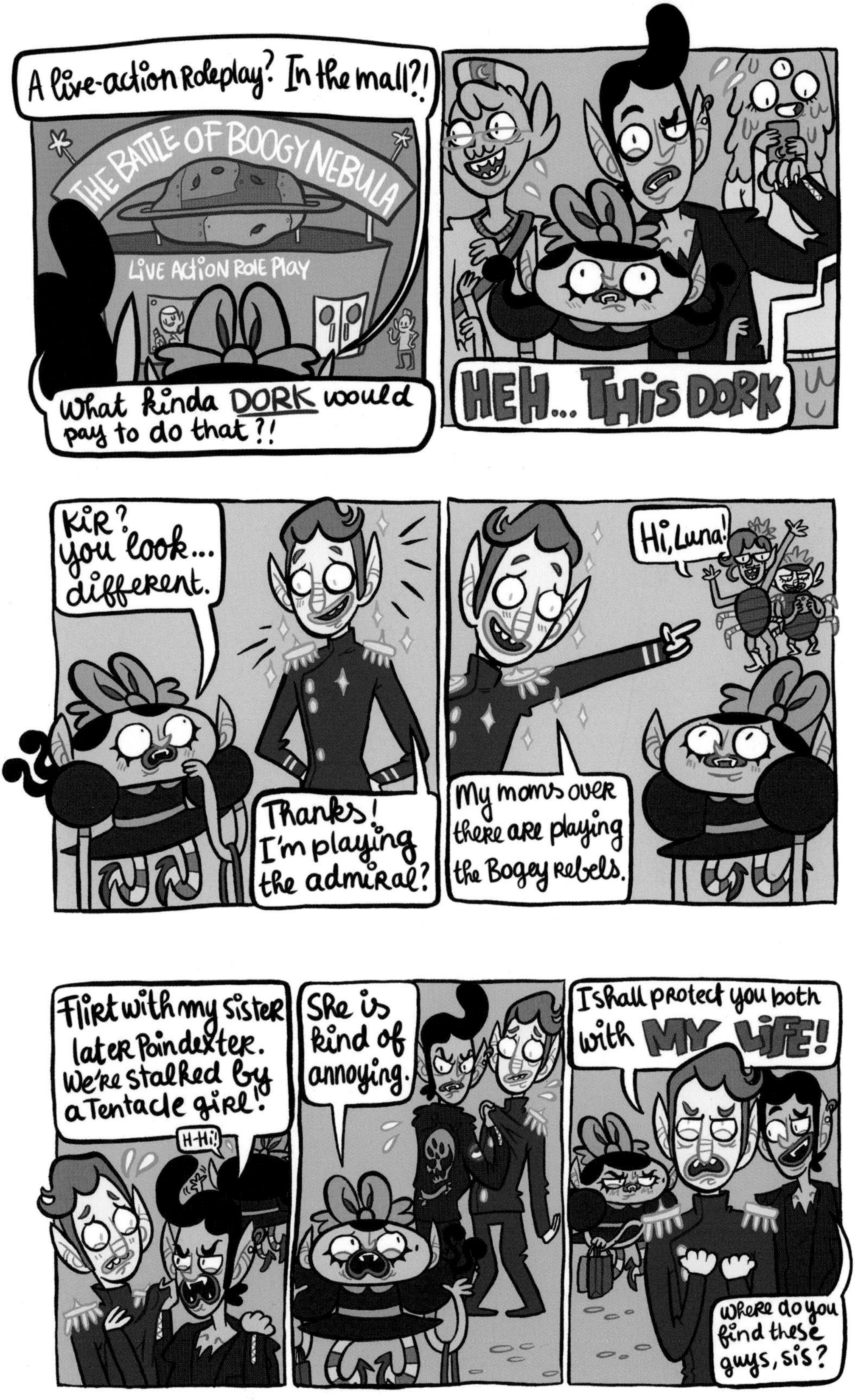
A live-action Roleplay? In the mall?!
THE BATTLE OF BOOGY NEBULA
LIVE ACTION ROLE PLAY
What kinda DORK would pay to do that?!
HEH... THIS DORK
Kir? you look... different.
Thanks! I'm playing the admiral?
My moms over there are playing the Bogey rebels.
Hi, Luna!
Flirt with my sister later Poindexter. We're stalked by a Tentacle girl!
H-Hi!
She is kind of annoying.
I shall protect you both with MY LIFE!
Where do you find these guys, sis?

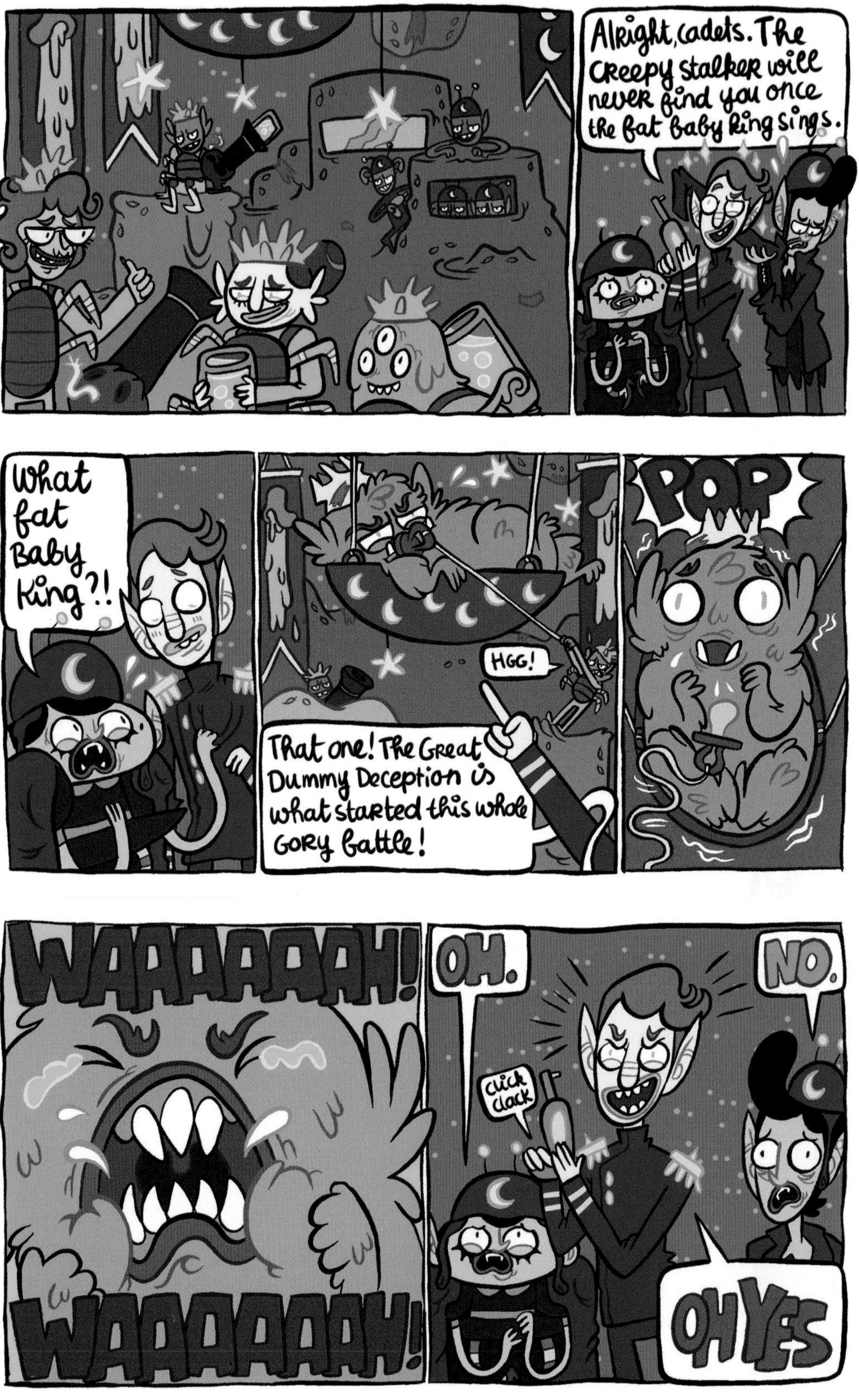
Alright, cadets. The creepy stalker will never find you once the fat baby king sings.
What fat Baby King?!
HGG!
That one! The Great Dummy Deception is what started this whole gory battle!
POP
WAAAAAAH!
WAAAAAAH!
OH.
NO.
click clack
OH YES

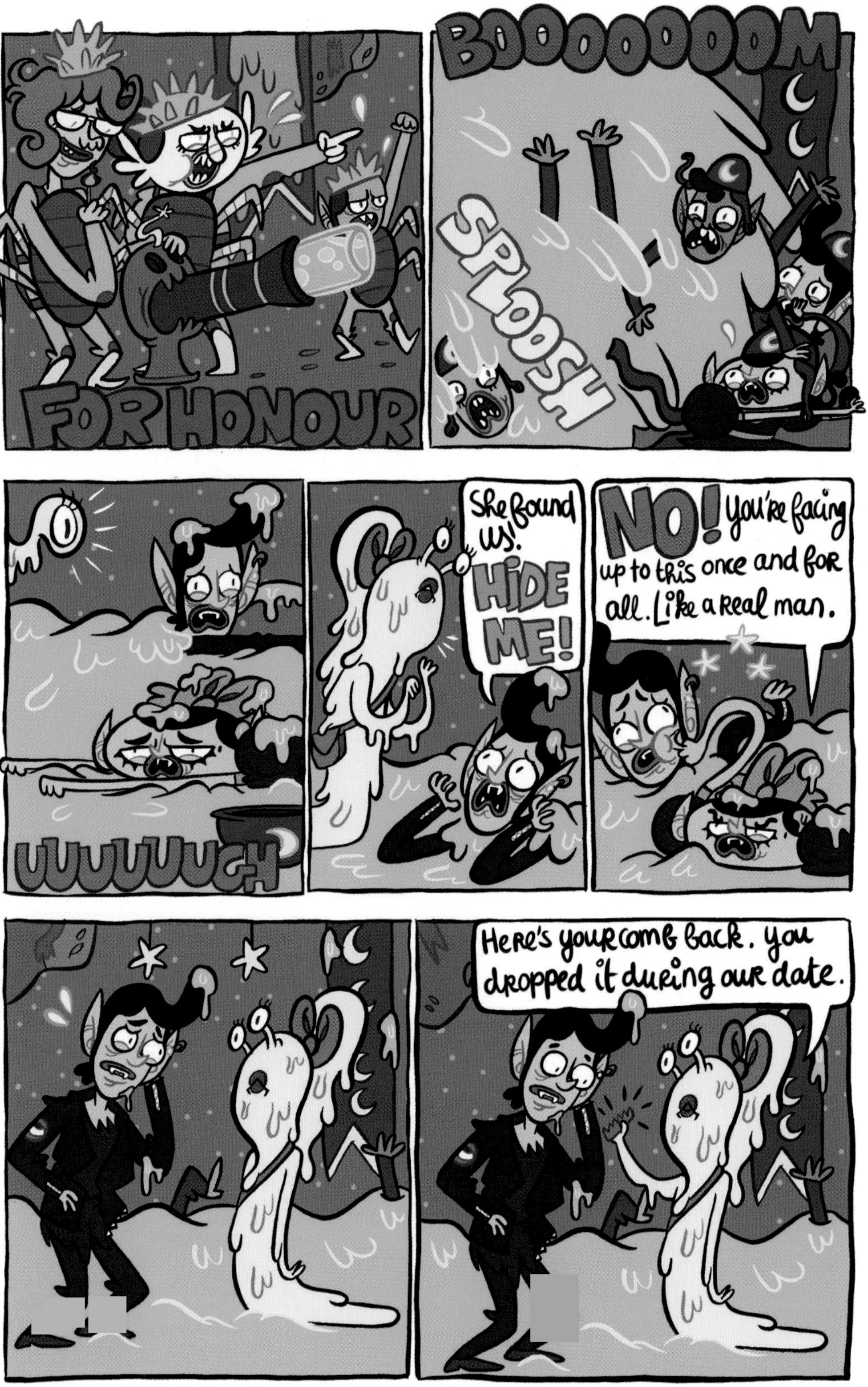
FOR HONOUR
BOOOOOOOOM
SPLOOSH
UUUUUUGH
She found us! HIDE ME!
NO! You're facing up to this once and for all. Like a real man.
Here's your comb back. You dropped it during our date.

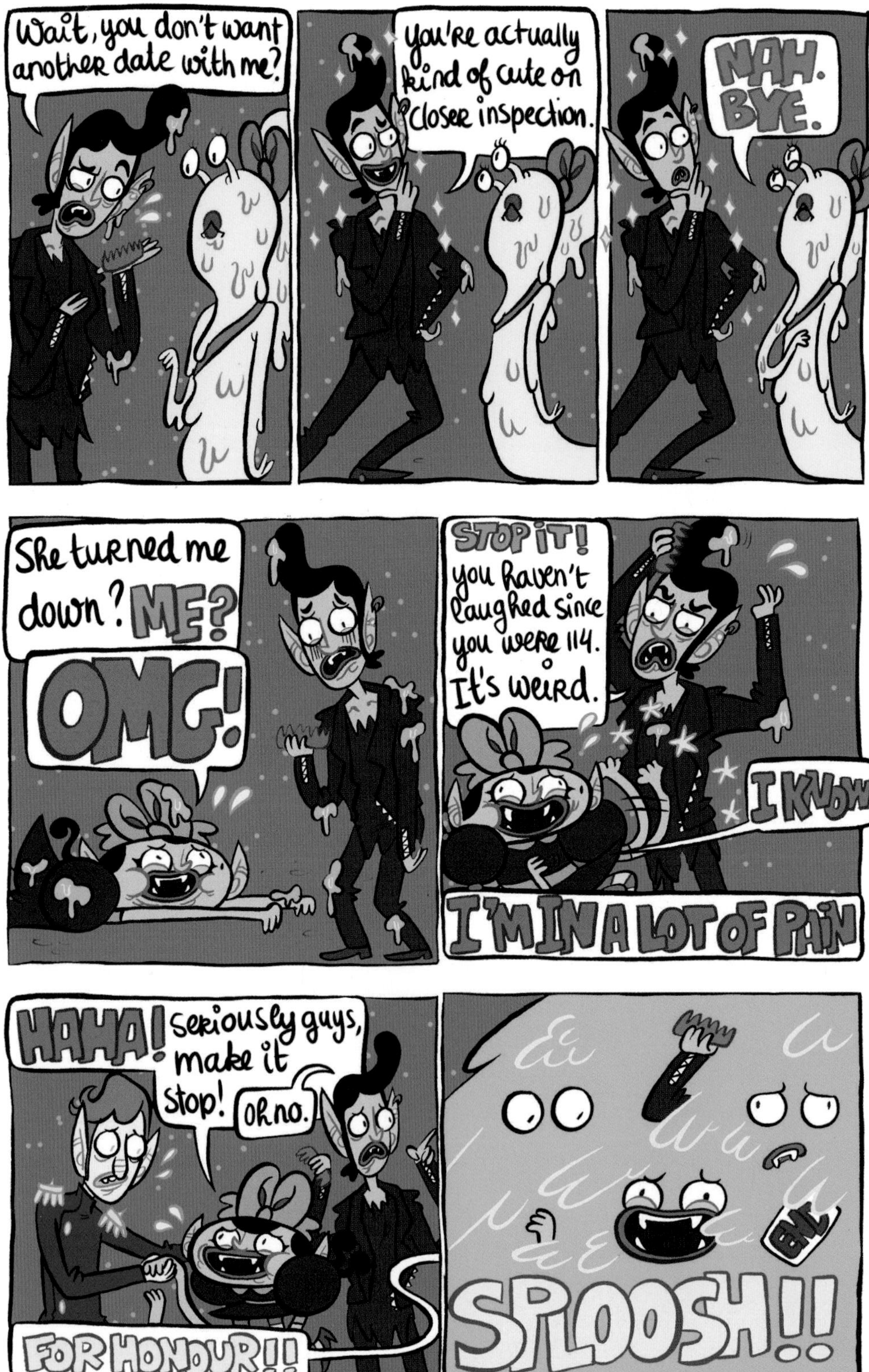
Wait, you don't want another date with me?
You're actually kind of cute on closer inspection.
NAH. BYE.
She turned me down? ME?
OMG!
STOP IT! you haven't laughed since you were 114. It's weird.
I KNOW
I'M IN A LOT OF PAIN
HAHA! seriously guys, make it stop!
Oh no.
FOR HONOUR!!
SPLOOSH!!

BAD WATER

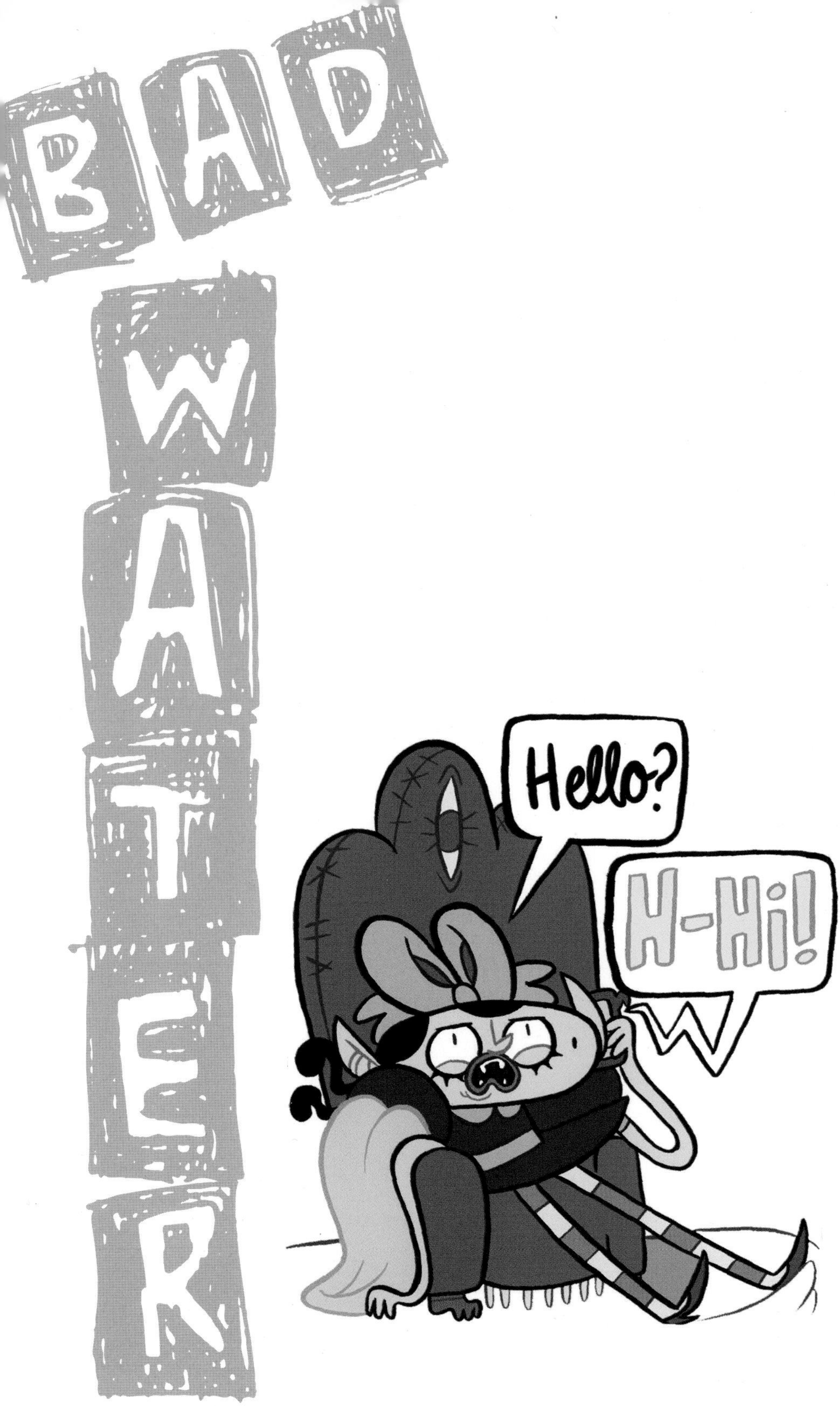
Hello?
H-Hi!

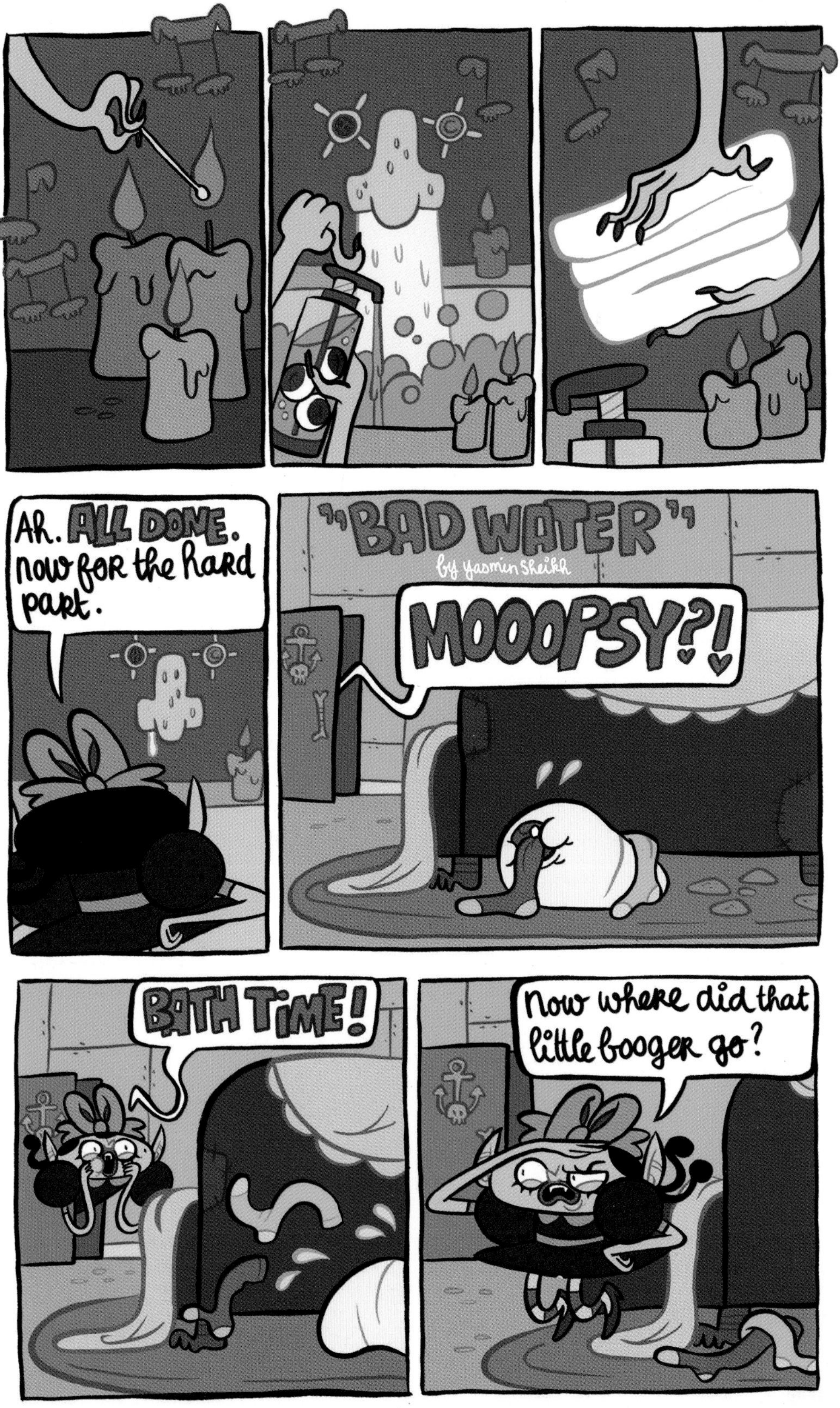
AH. ALL DONE. now for the hard part.
"BAD WATER"
by yasmin sheikh
MOOOPSY?!
BATH TIME!
now where did that little booger go?

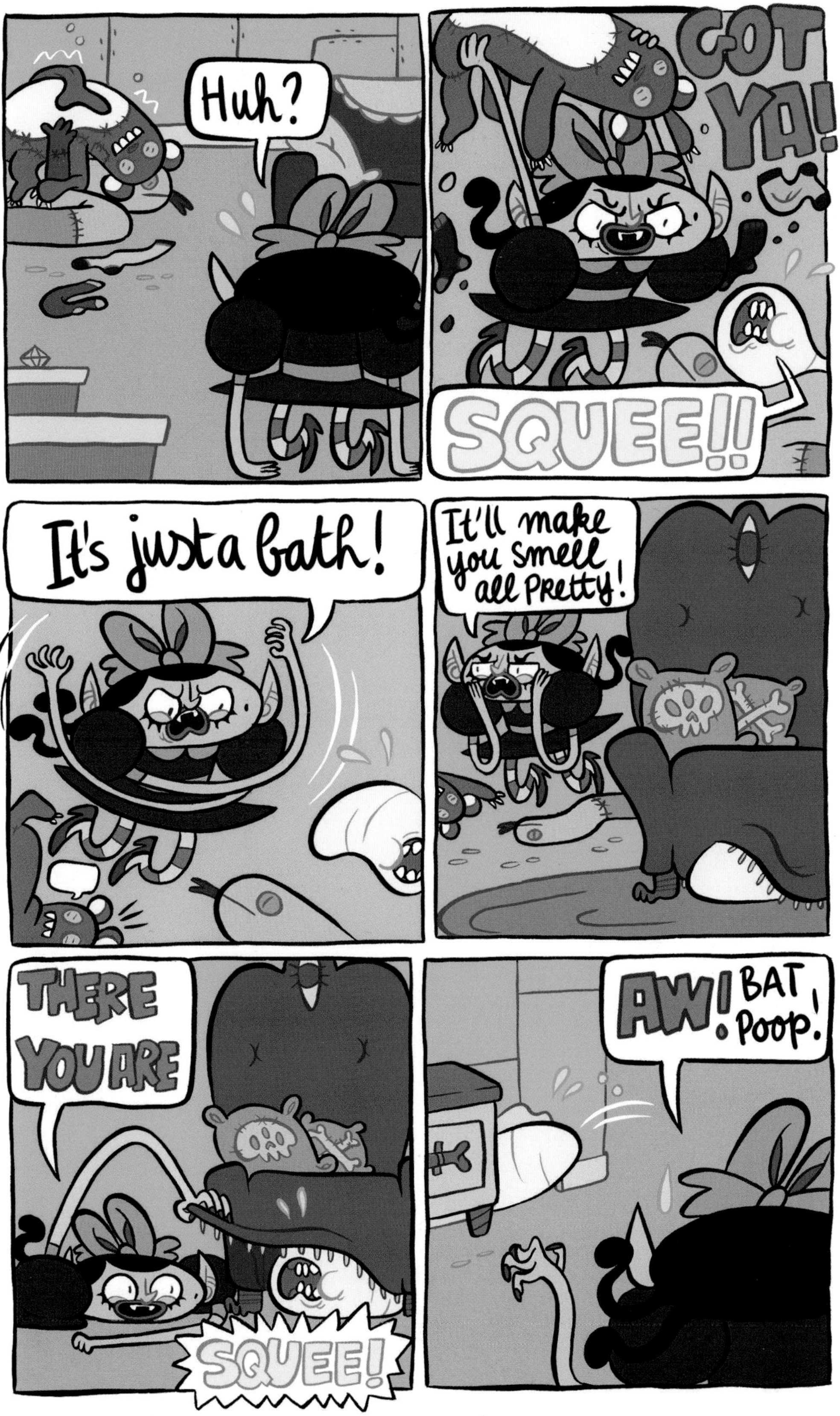
Huh?
GOT YA!
SQUEE!!
It's just a bath!
It'll make you smell all Pretty!
THERE YOU ARE
SQUEE!
AW! BAT Poop!

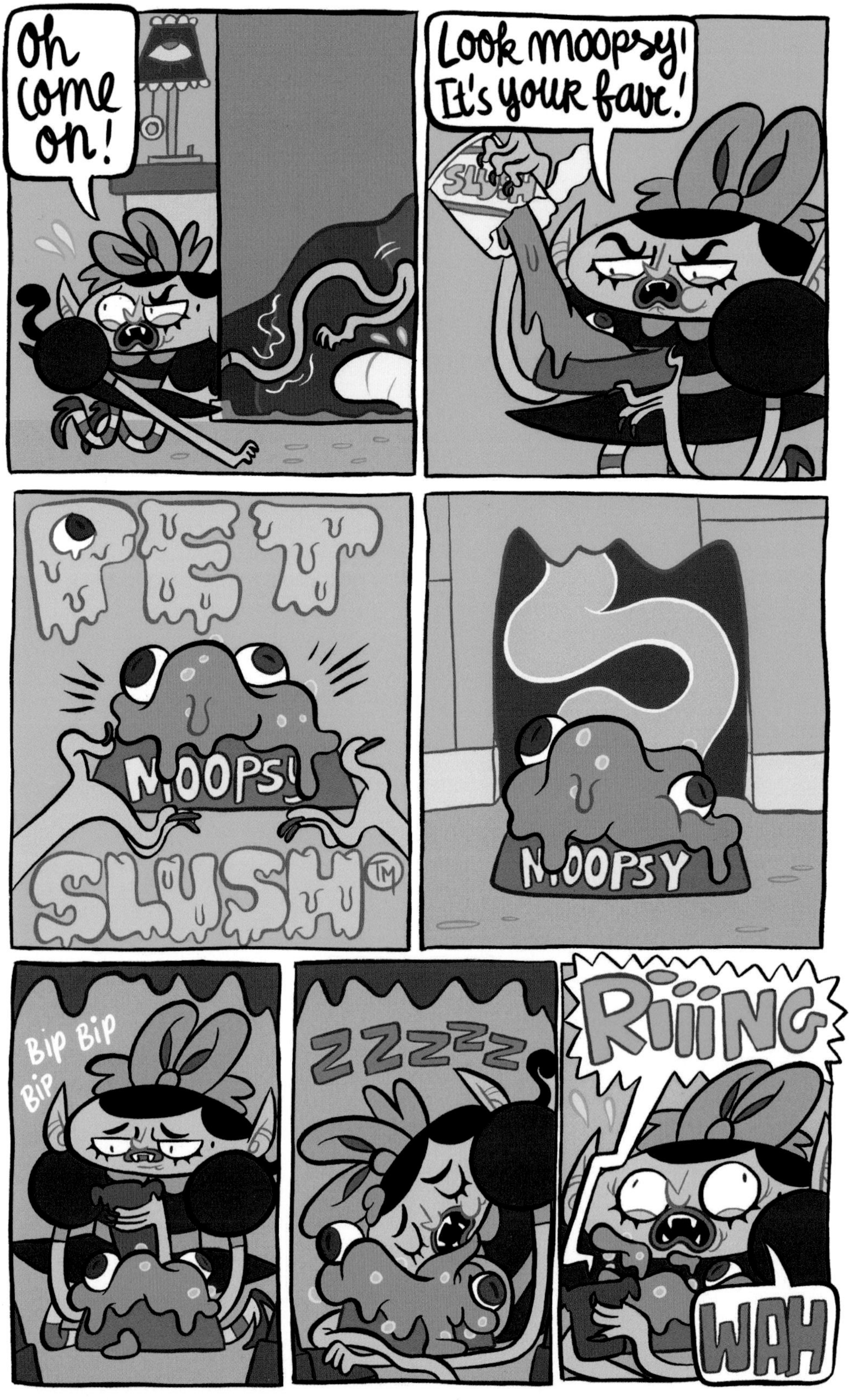
Oh come on!
Look moopsy! It's your fave!
SLUSH
PET SLUSH™
MOOPSY
MOOPSY
Bip Bip Bip
ZZZZZ
RIIING
WAH

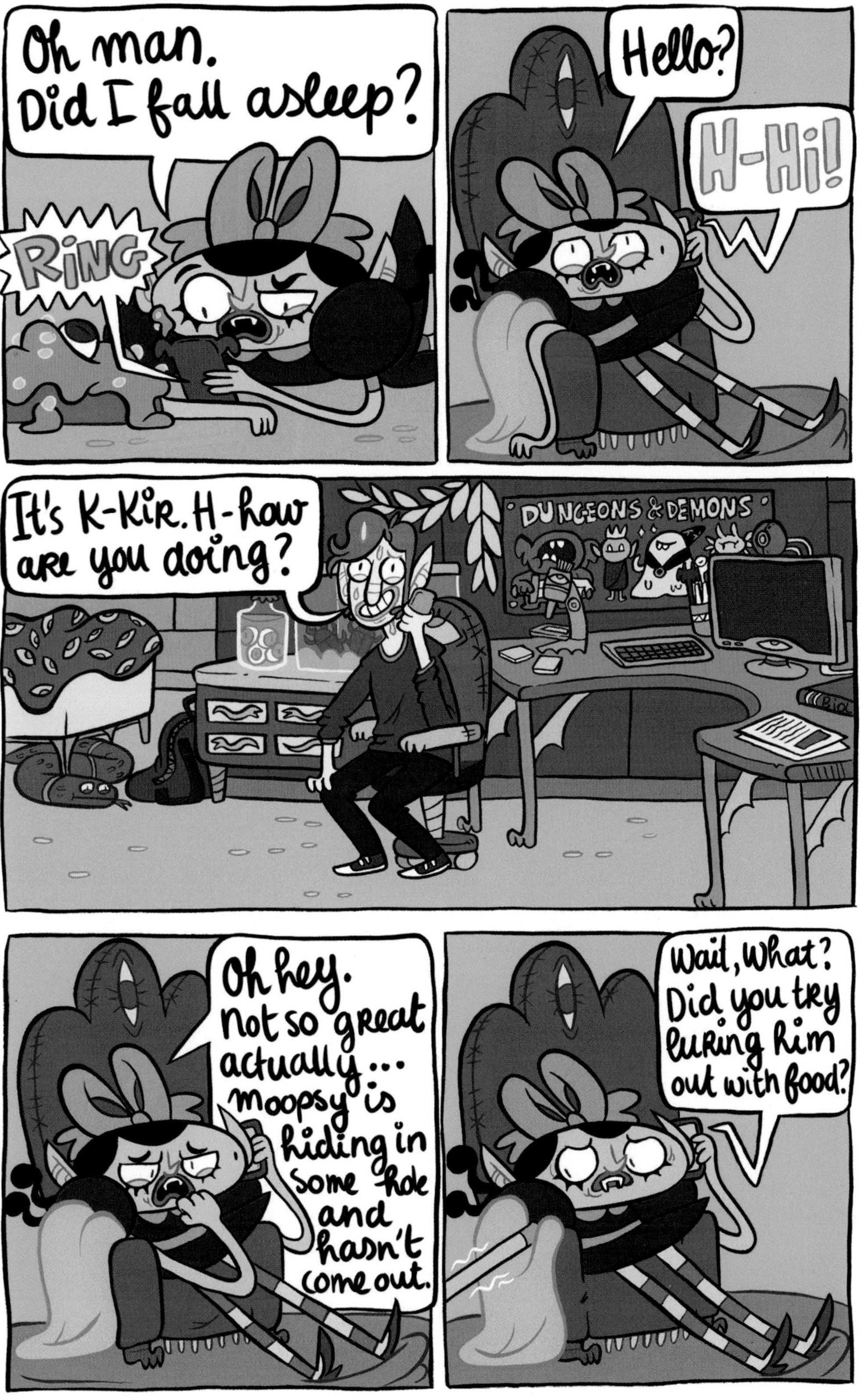
Oh man.
Did I fall asleep?
RING
Hello?
H-Hi!
It's K-Kir. H-how are you doing?
DUNGEONS & DEMONS
Oh hey.
not so great actually... moopsy is hiding in some hole and hasn't come out.
Wait, What? Did you try luring him out with food?

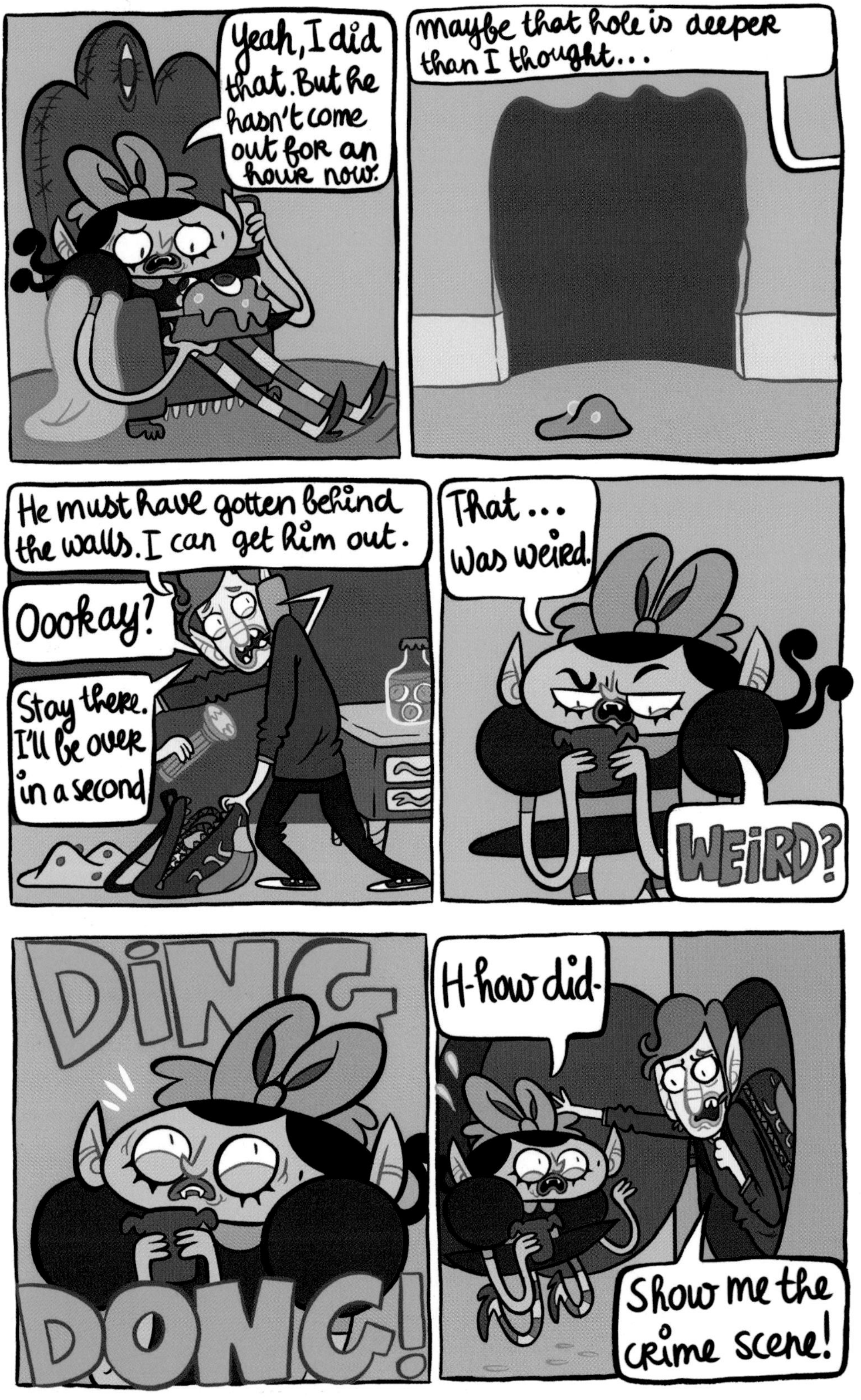
Yeah, I did that. But he hasn't come out for an hour now.
maybe that hole is deeper than I thought...
He must have gotten behind the walls. I can get him out.
Oookay?
Stay there. I'll be over in a second
That... Was weird.
WEIRD?
DING
DONG!
H-how did-
Show me the crime scene!

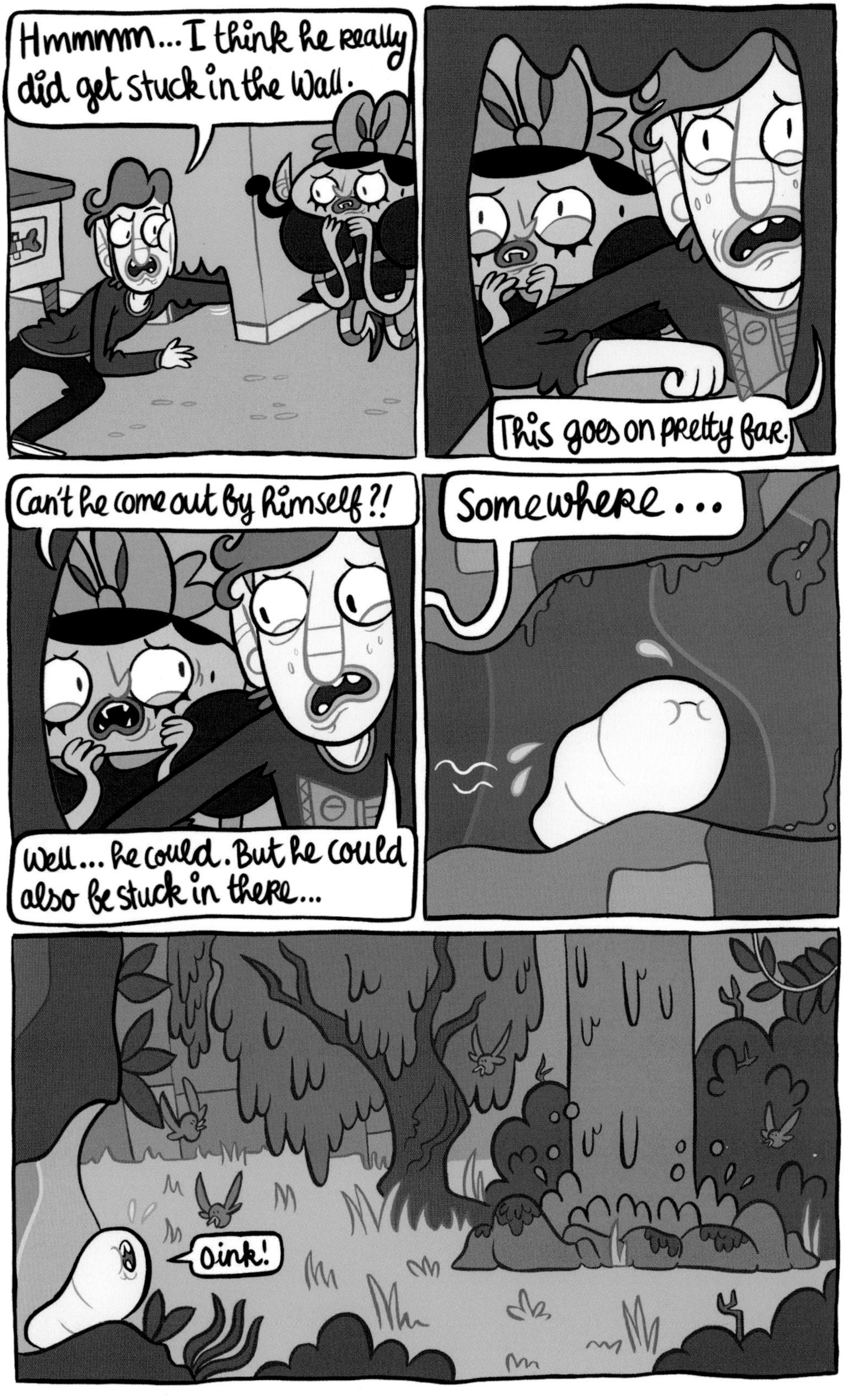
Hmmmm... I think he really did get stuck in the wall.
This goes on pretty far.
Can't he come out by himself?!
Well... he could. But he could also be stuck in there...
Somewhere...
Oink!

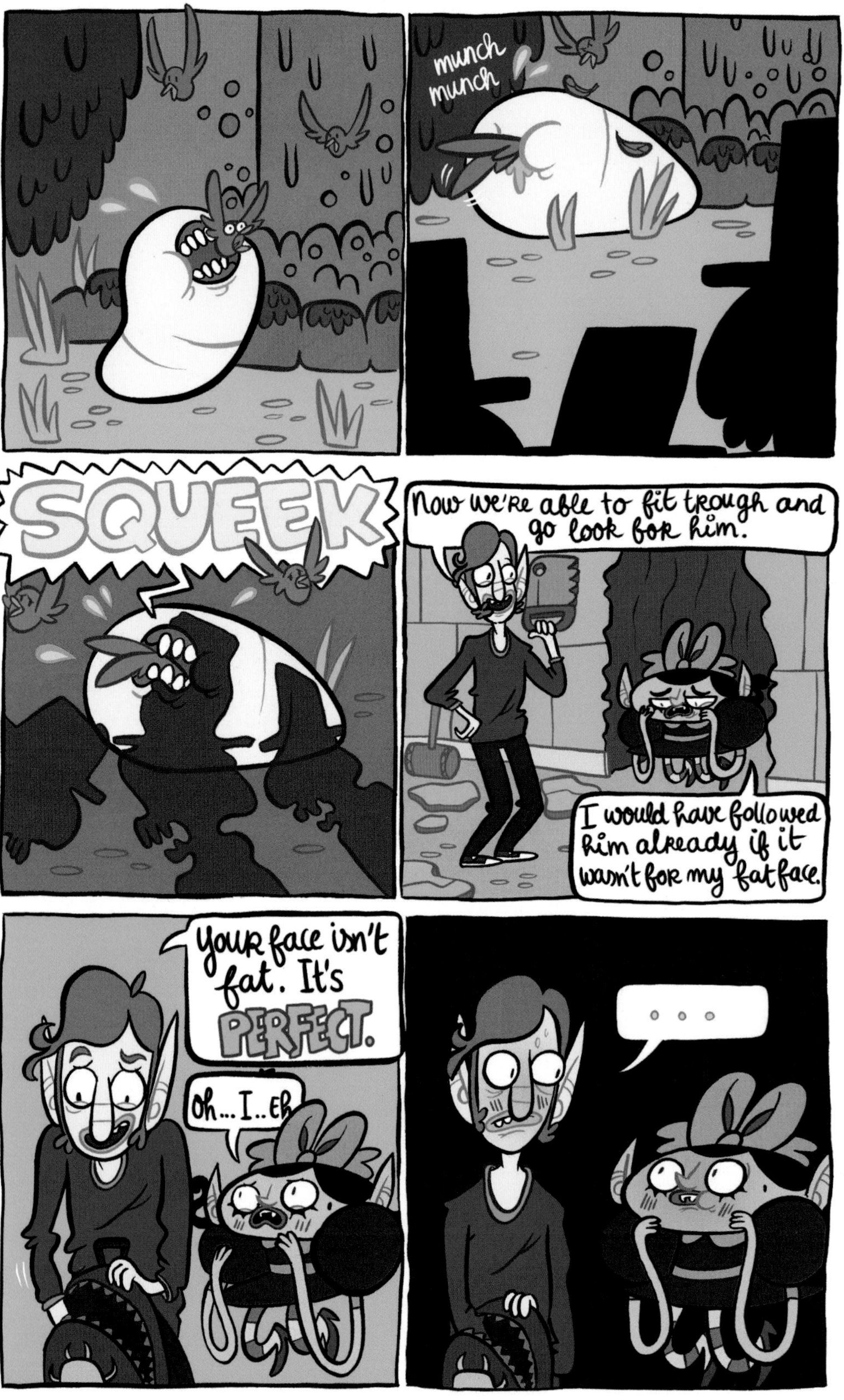
munch
munch
SQUEEK
Now we're able to fit trough and go look for him.
I would have followed him already if it wasn't for my fat face.
Your face isn't fat. It's PERFECT.
Oh... I.. Eh
. . .

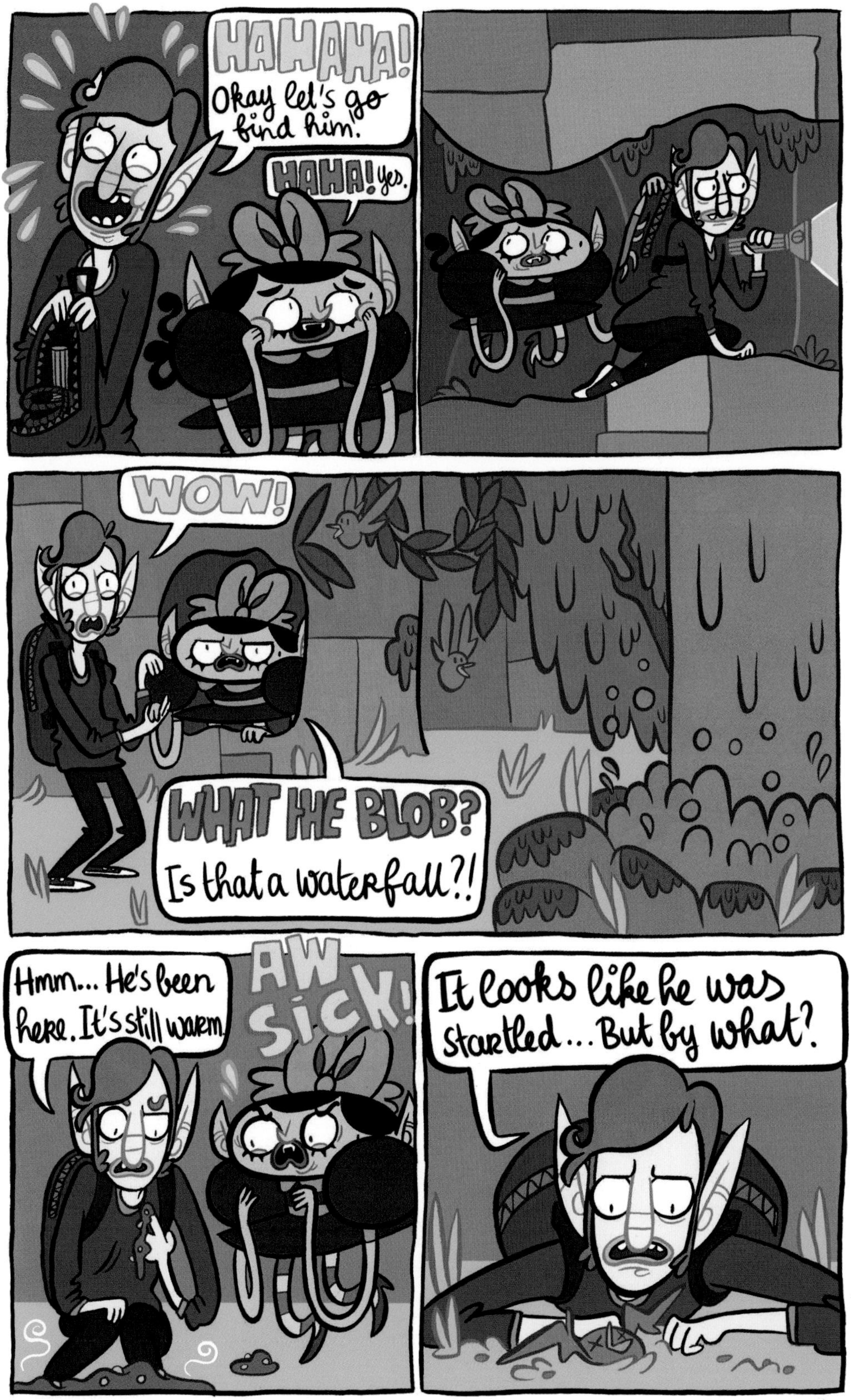
HAHAHA! Okay let's go find him!
HAHA! yes.
WOW!
WHAT THE BLOB? Is that a waterfall?!
Hmm... He's been here. It's still warm.
AW SICK!
It looks like he was startled... But by what?

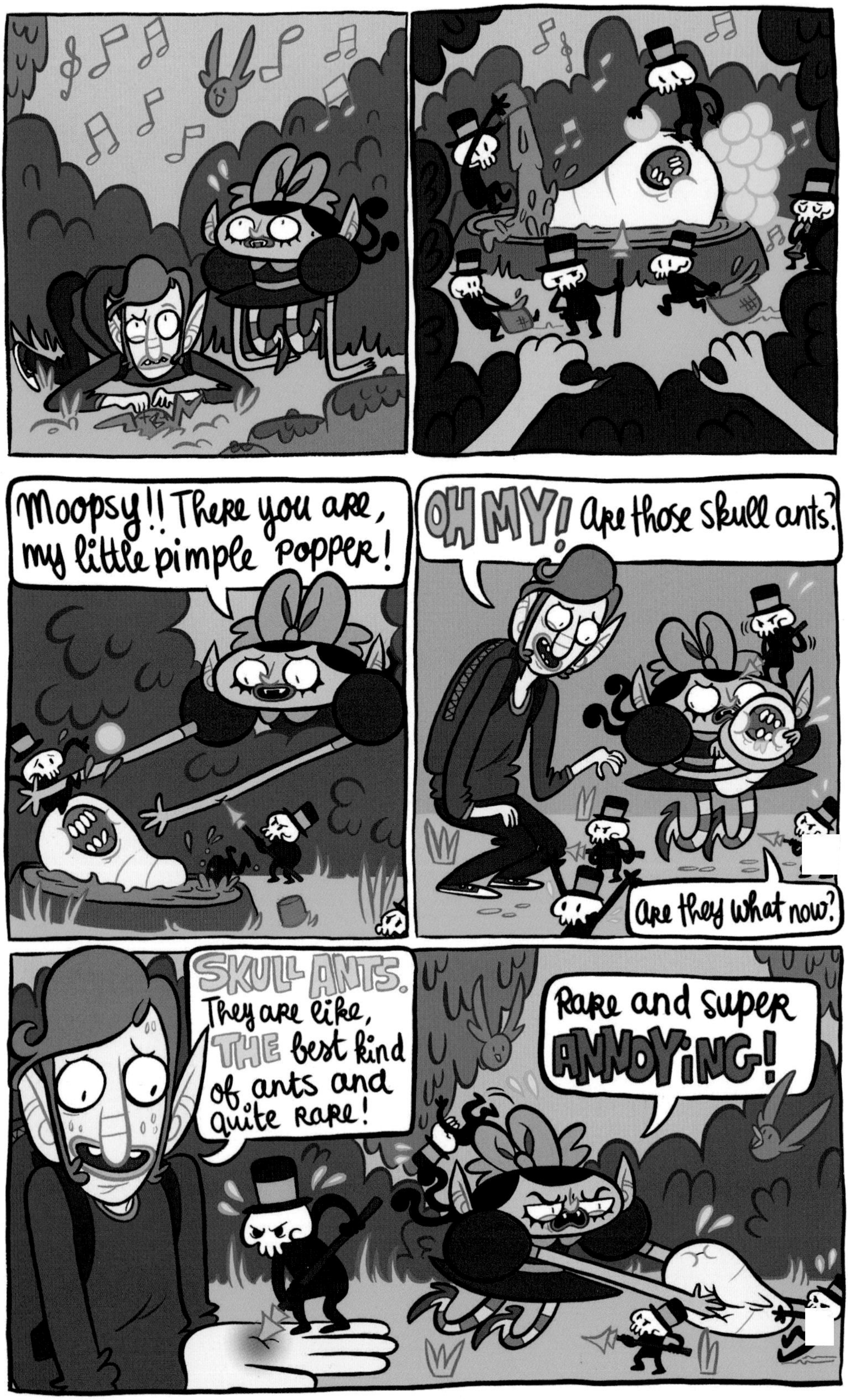
Moopsy!! There you are, my little pimple popper!
OH MY! Are those skull ants?
Are they what now?
SKULL ANTS. They are like, THE best kind of ants and quite rare!
Rare and super ANNOYING!

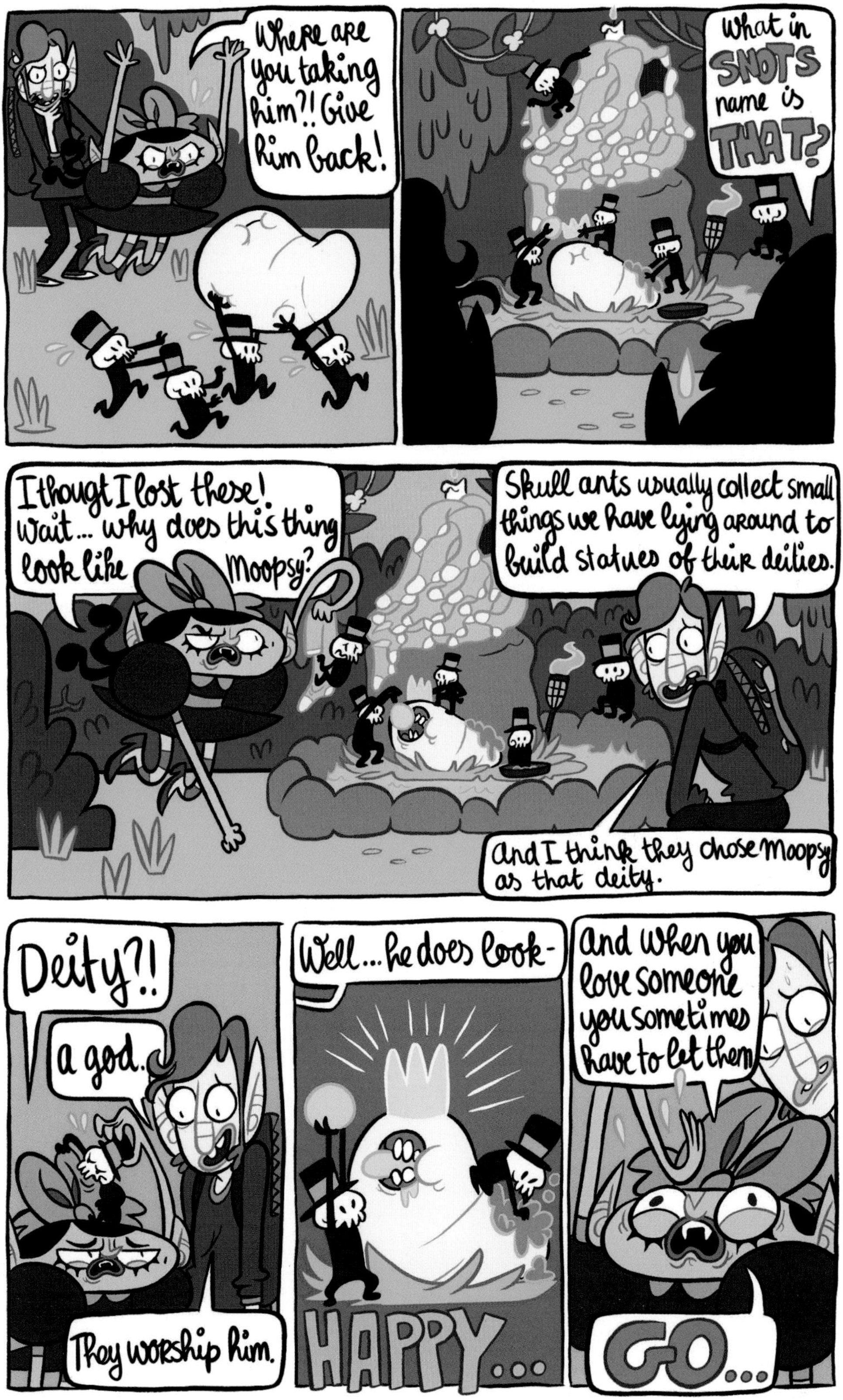
Where are you taking him?!. Give him back!
What in SNOTS name is THAT?
I thougt I lost these! Wait... why does this thing look like Moopsy?
Skull ants usually collect small things we have lying around to build statues of their deities.
And I think they chose Moopsy as that deity.
Deity?!.
a god.
They worship him.
Well... he does look-
HAPPY...
And when you love someone you sometimes have to let them
GO...

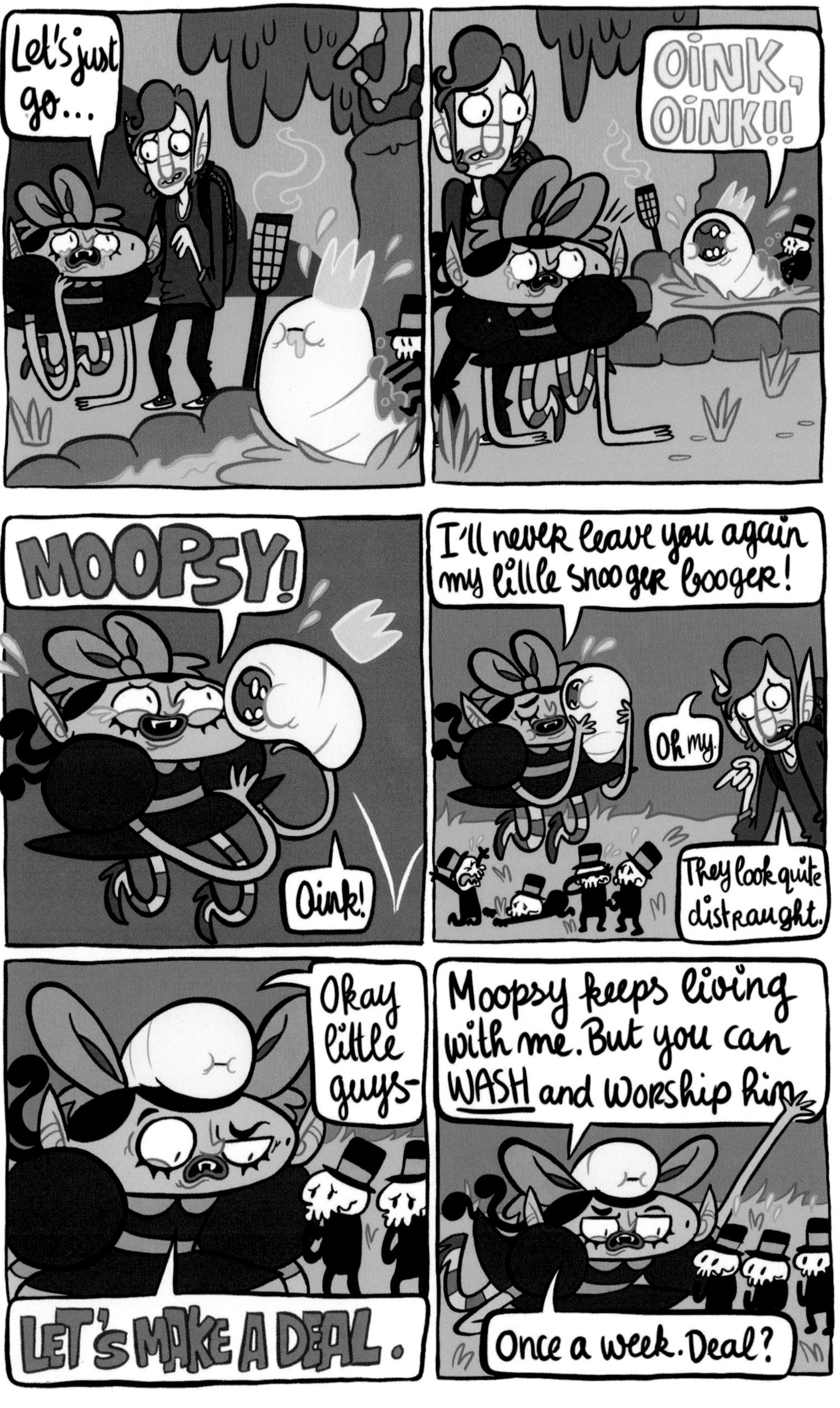

Let's just go...
OINK, OINK!!
MOOPSY!
Oink!
I'll never leave you again my little snooger booger!
Oh my.
They look quite distraught.
Okay little guys-
LET'S MAKE A DEAL.
Moopsy keeps living with me. But you can WASH and worship him
Once a week. Deal?

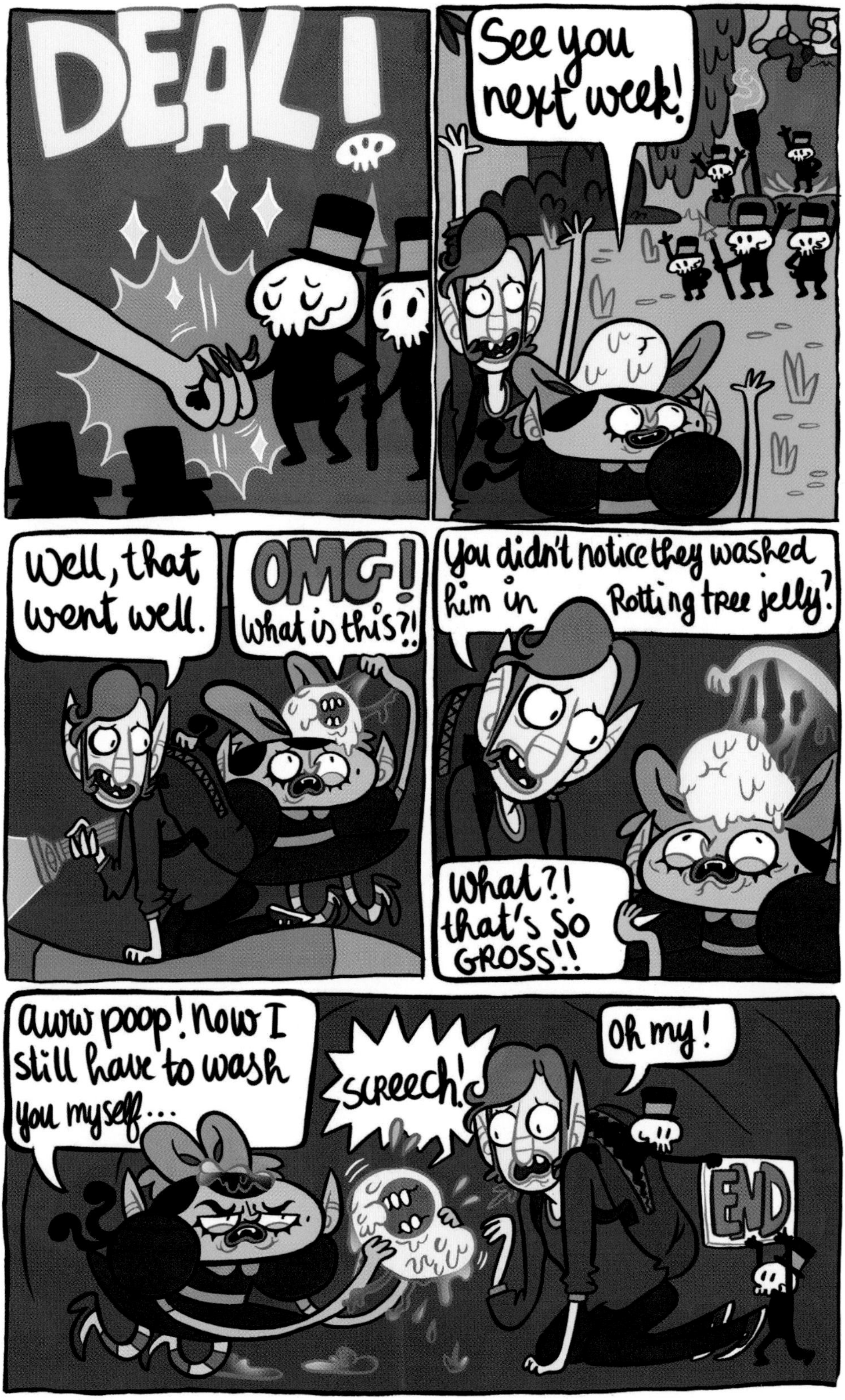
DEAL!
See you next week!
Well, that went well.
OMG! What is this?!
You didn't notice they washed him in Rotting tree jelly?
What?! that's SO GROSS!!
aww poop! now I still have to wash you myself...
SCREECH!
Oh my!
END

SURVIVAL OF THE SUCKIEST

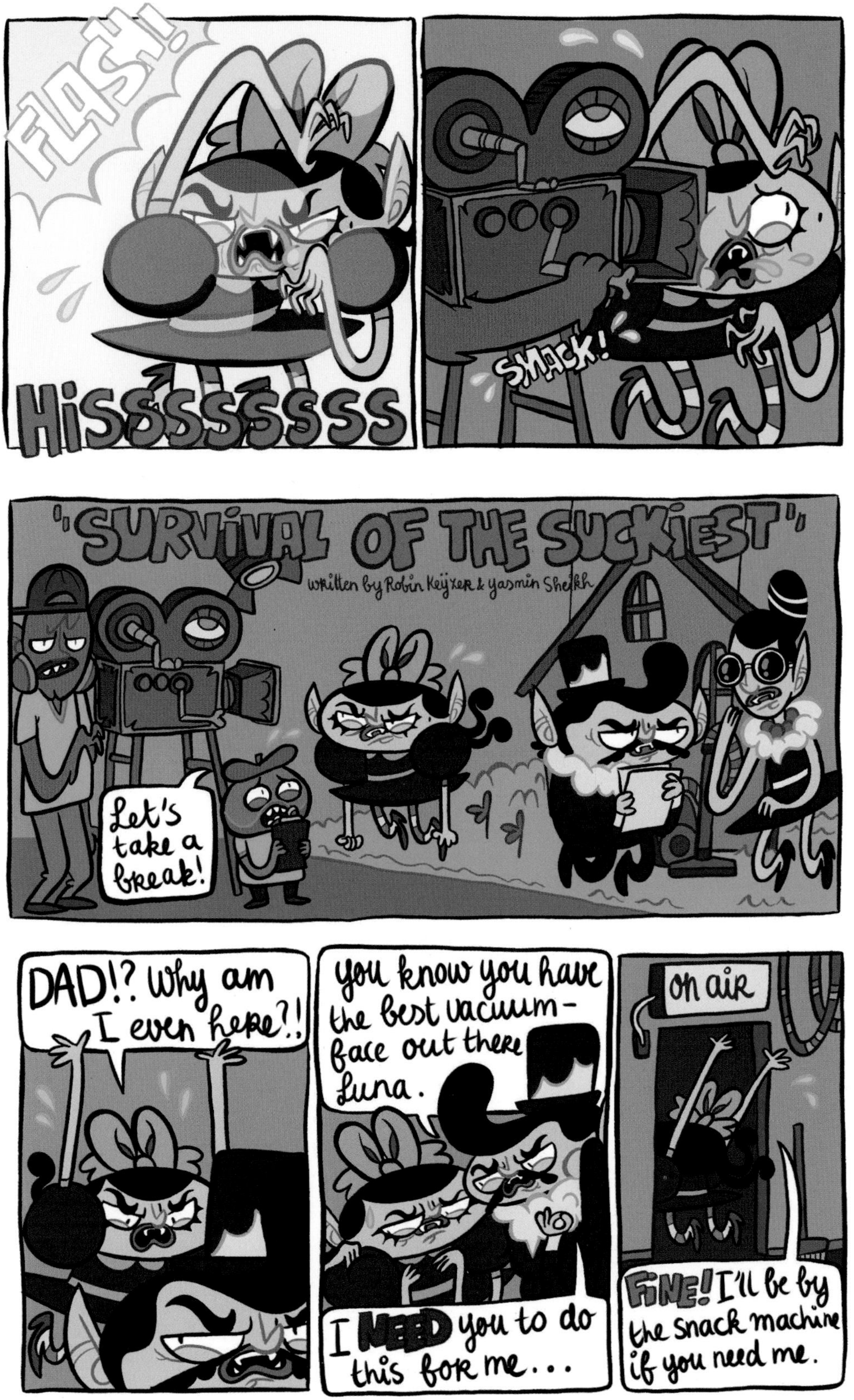
FLASH!
HISSSSSSSS
SMACK!
"SURVIVAL OF THE SUCKIEST"
written by Robin Keijzer & Yasmin Sheikh
Let's take a break!
DAD!? Why am I even here?!
You know you have the best vacuum-face out there Luna.
I NEED you to do this for me...
ON AIR
FINE! I'll be by the snack machine if you need me.

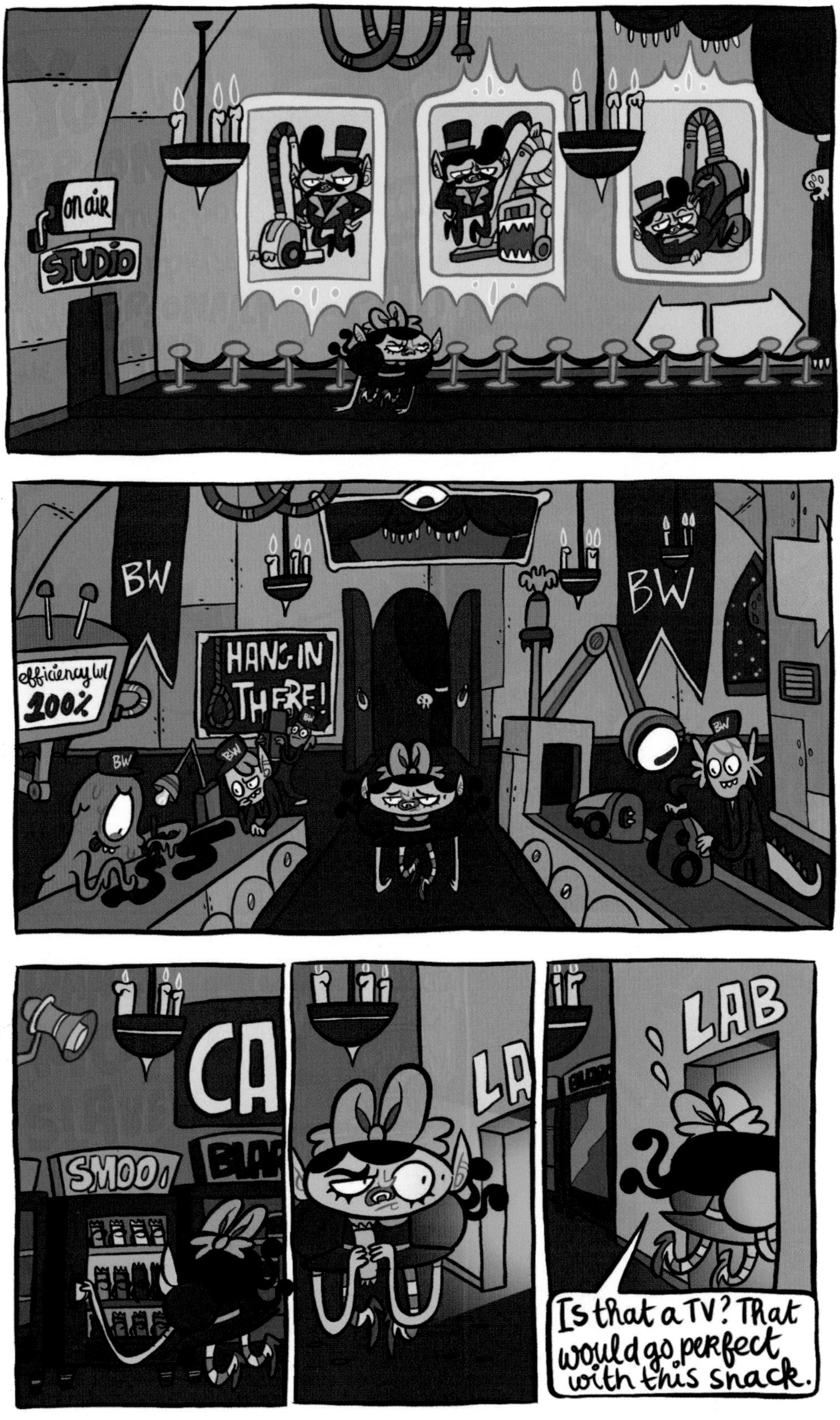
on air
STUDIO
BW
efficiency lvl
100%
HANG IN THERE!
BW
CA
SMOO
LA
LAB
Is that a TV? That would go perfect with this snack.

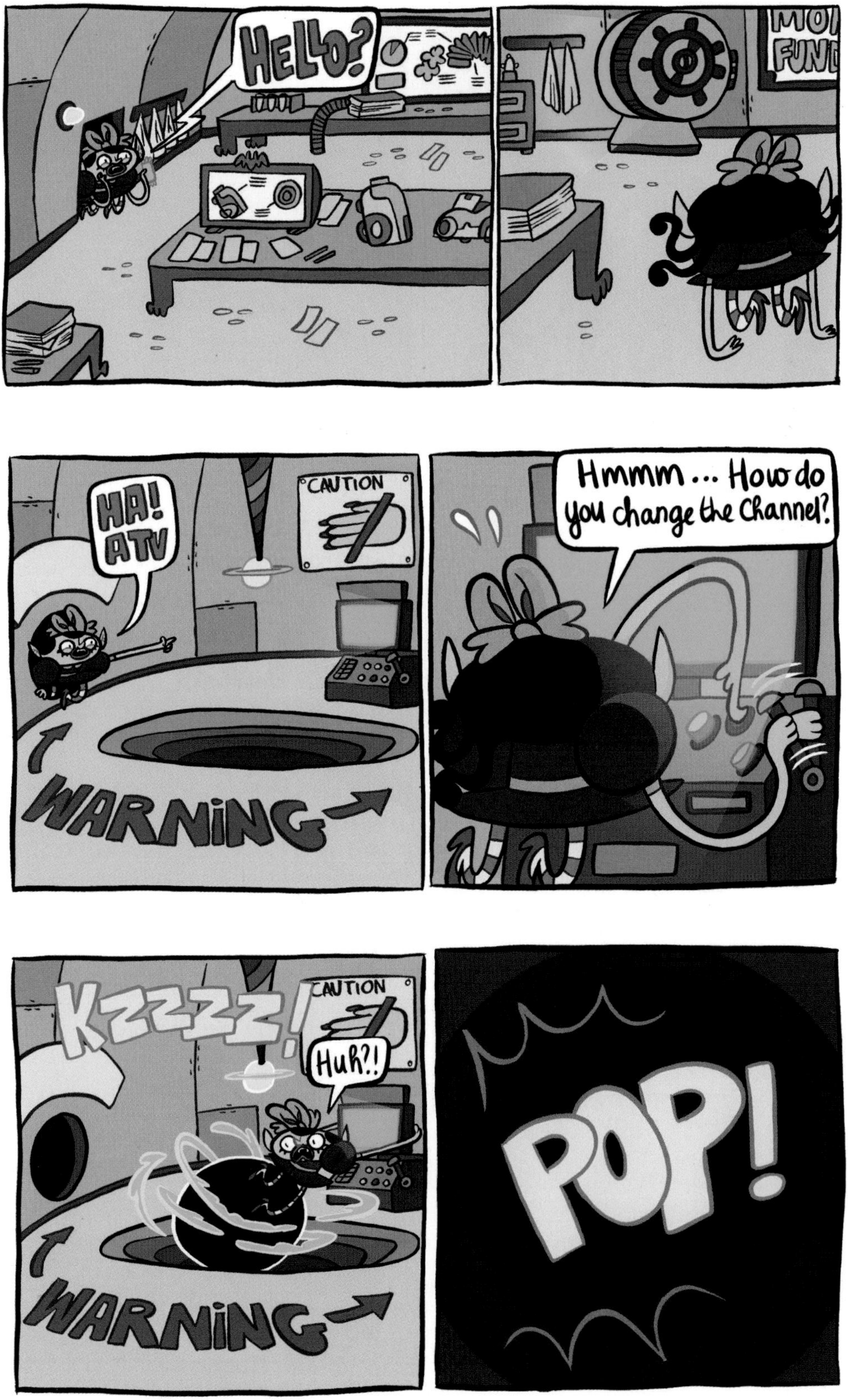

HELLO?
MO
FUND
HA! A TV
CAUTION
WARNING
Hmmm... How do you change the Channel?
KZZZZ!
CAUTION
Huh?!
WARNING
POP!

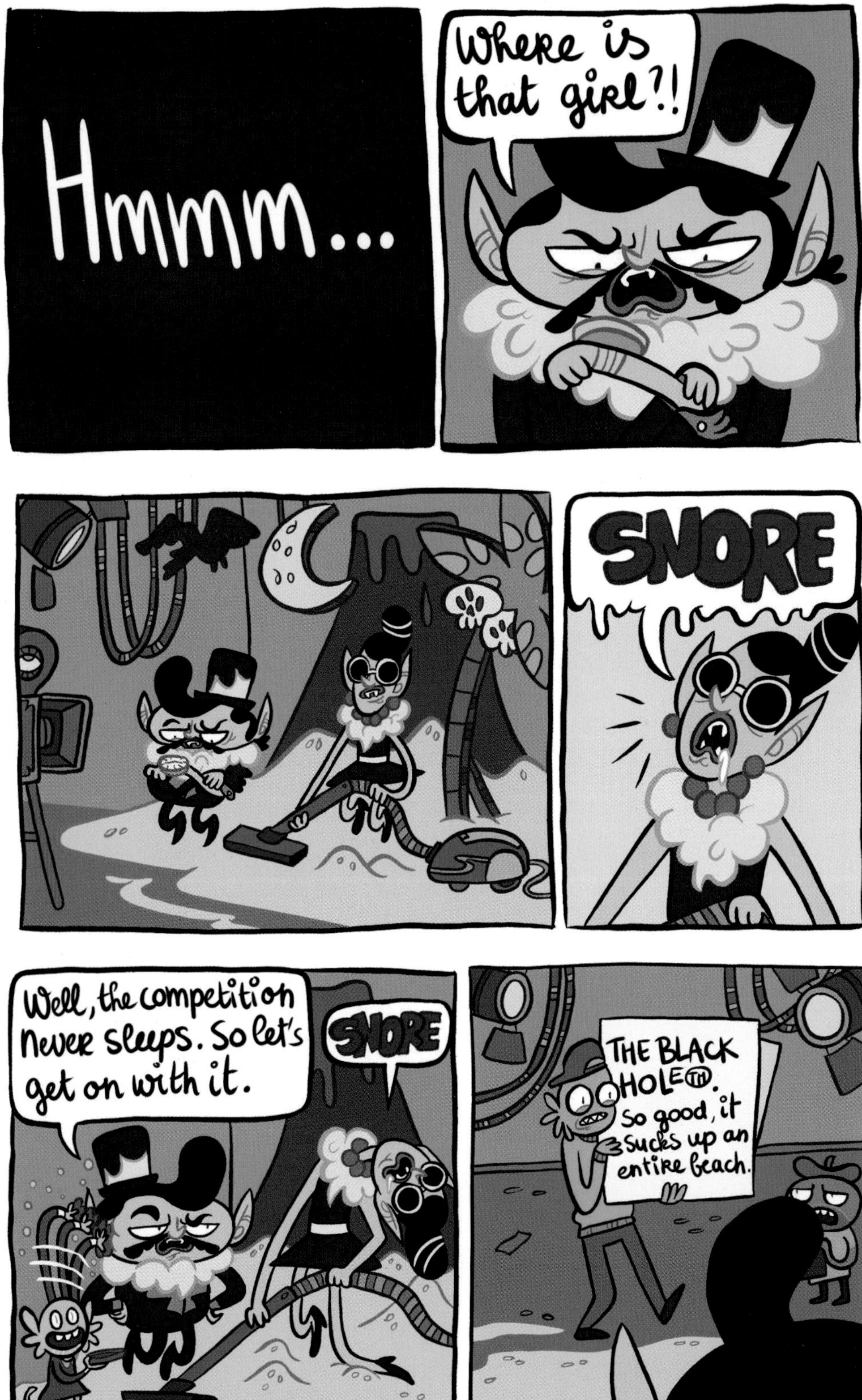
Hmmm...
Where is that girl?!
SNORE
Well, the competition never sleeps. So let's get on with it.
SNORE
THE BLACK HOLE™. So good, it sucks up an entire beach.

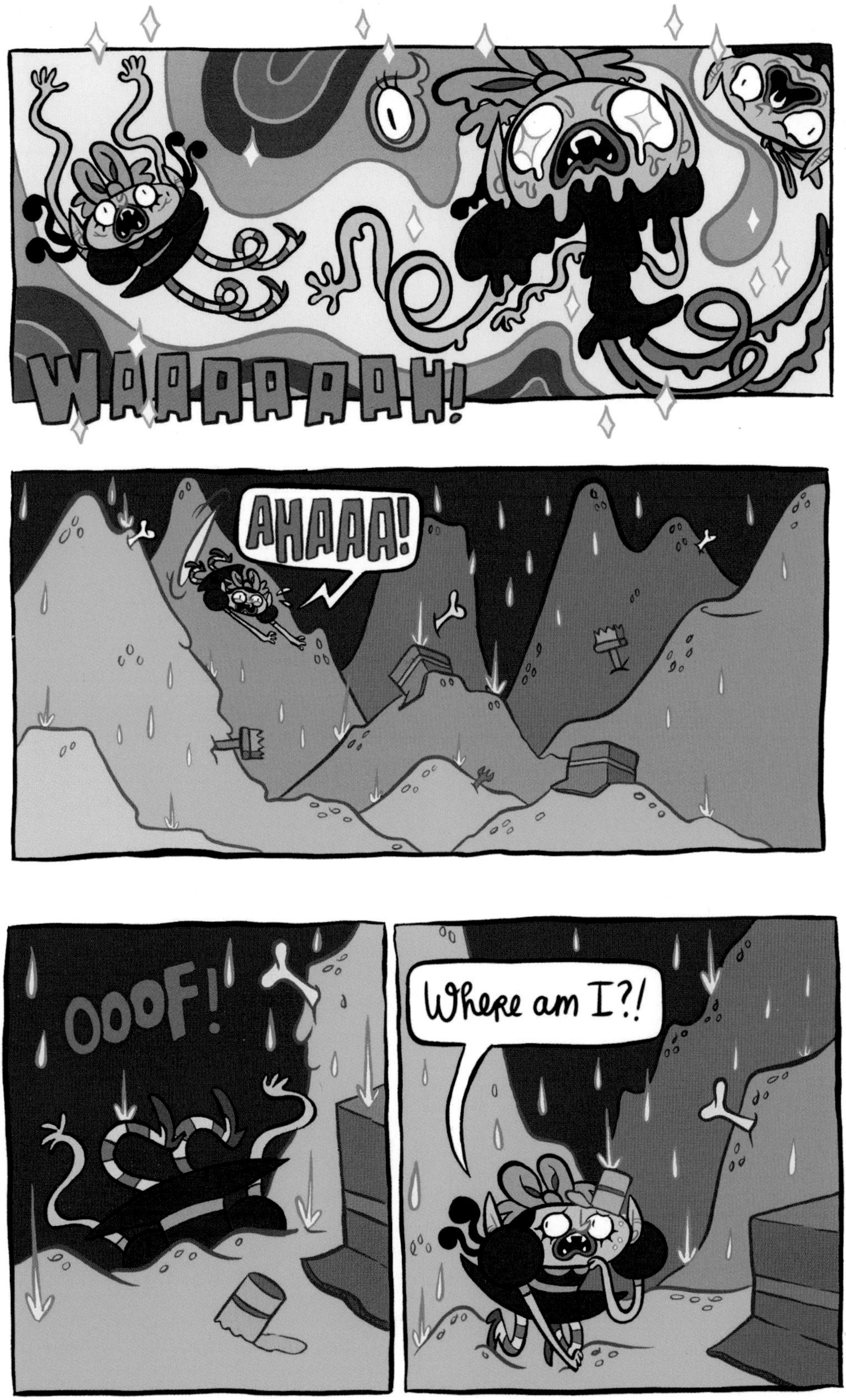
WAAAAAAAH!
AHAAAA!
OOOF!
Where am I?!

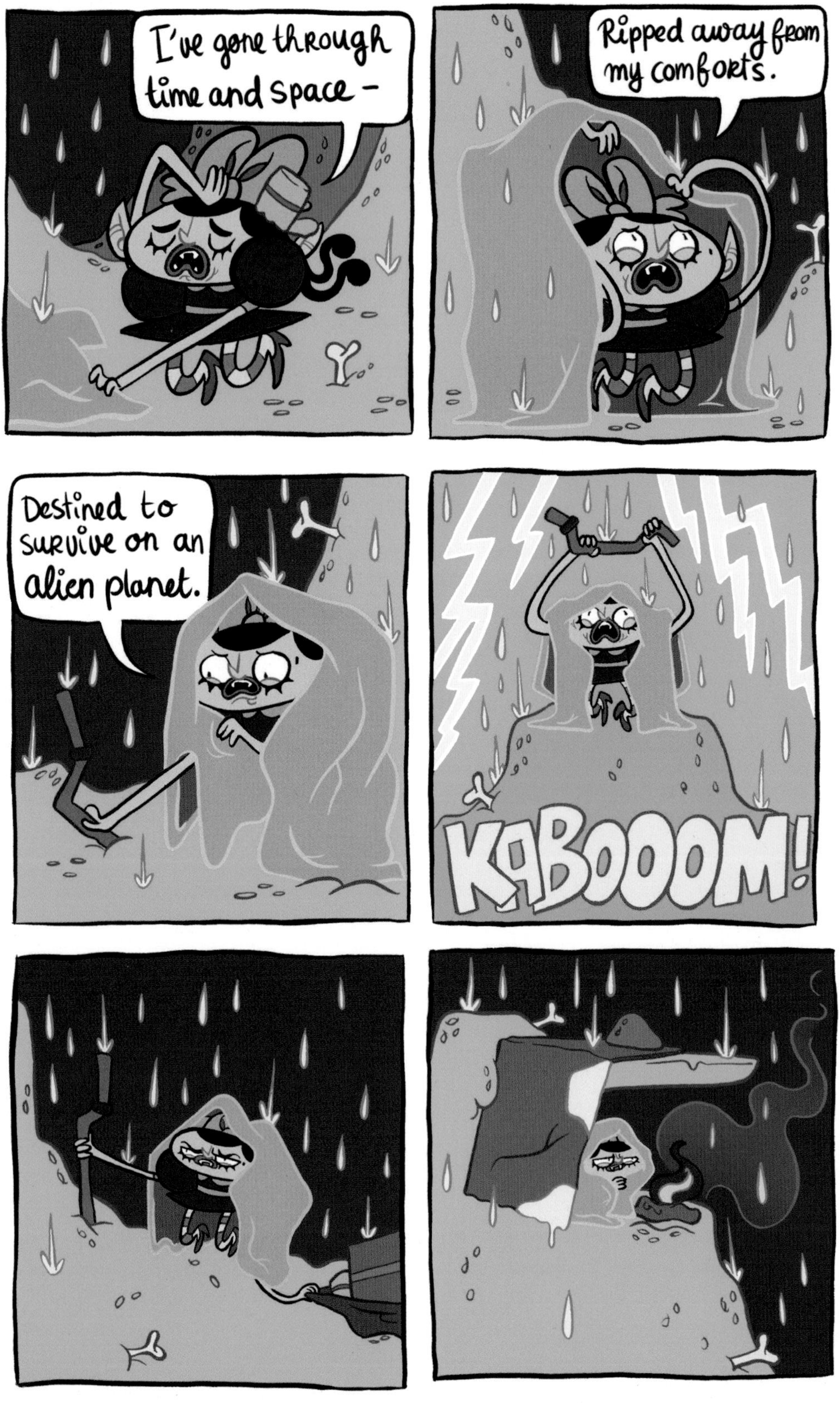
I've gone through time and space -
Ripped away from my comforts.
Destined to survive on an alien planet.
KABOOOM!

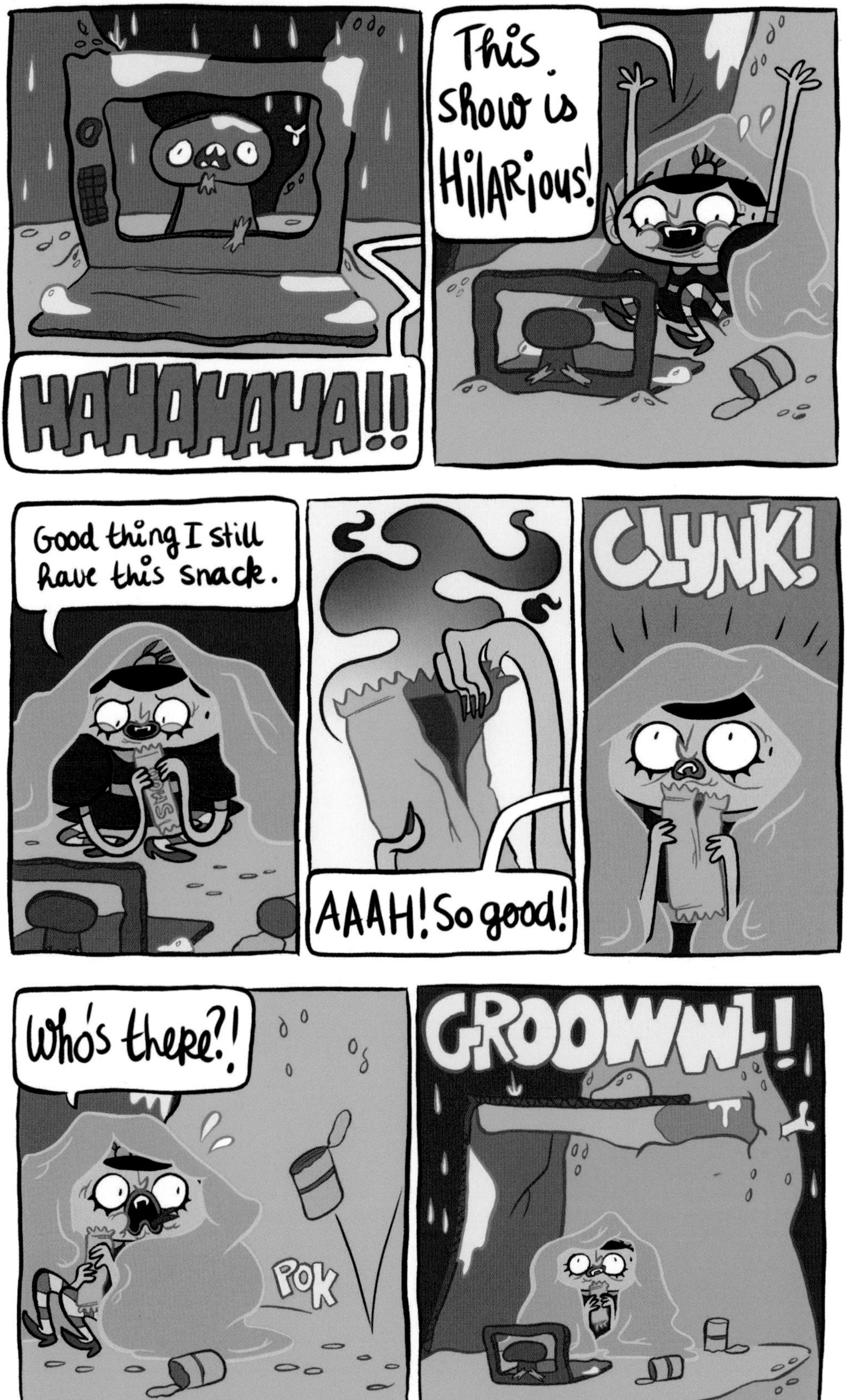
HAHAHAHA!!
This show is Hilarious!
Good thing I still have this snack.
AAAH! So good!
CLYNK!
Who's there?!
POK
GROOWNL!

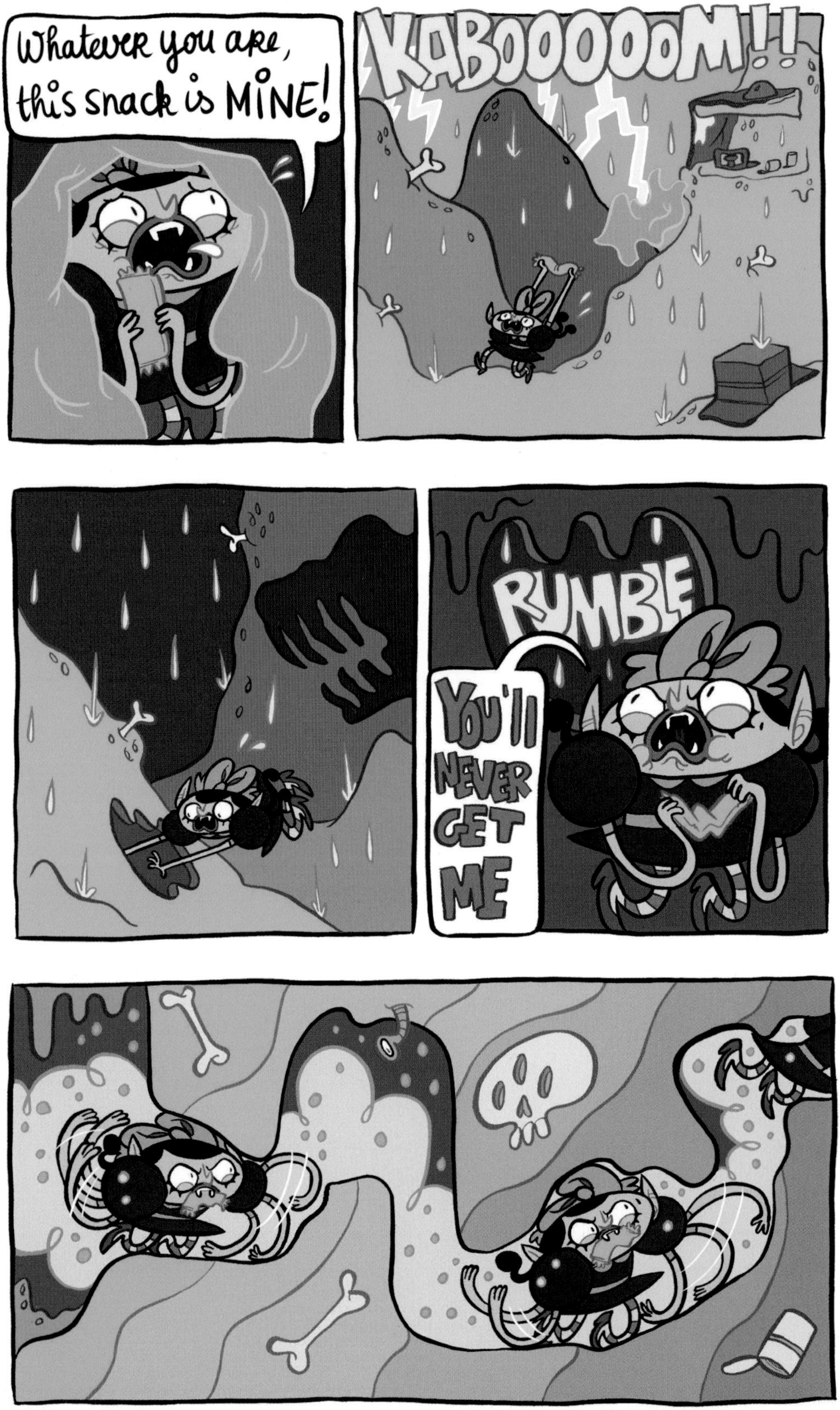
Whatever you are, this snack is MINE!
KABOOOOOOM!!
RUMBLE
YOU'LL NEVER GET ME

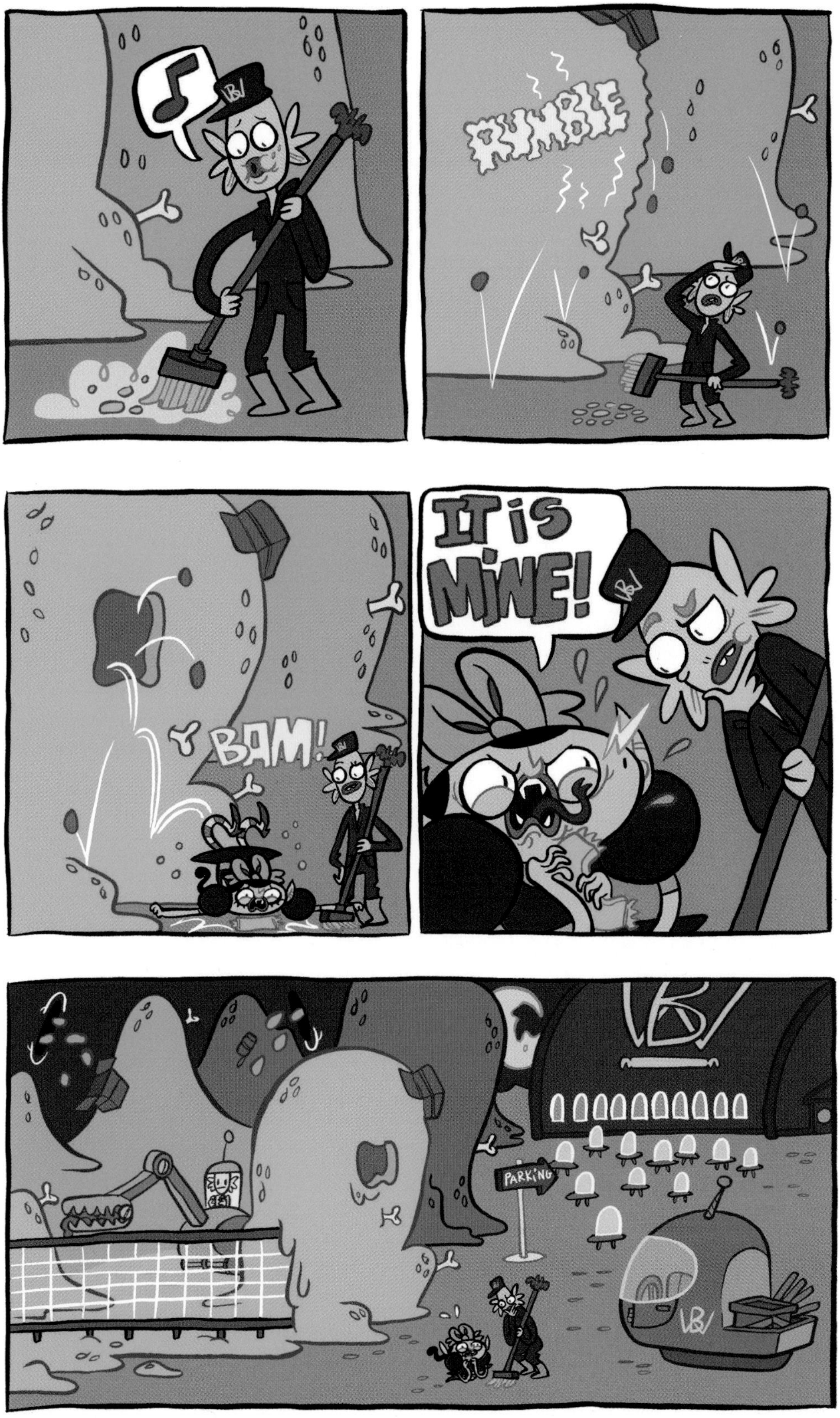
RUMBLE
BAM!
IT IS MINE!
PARKING

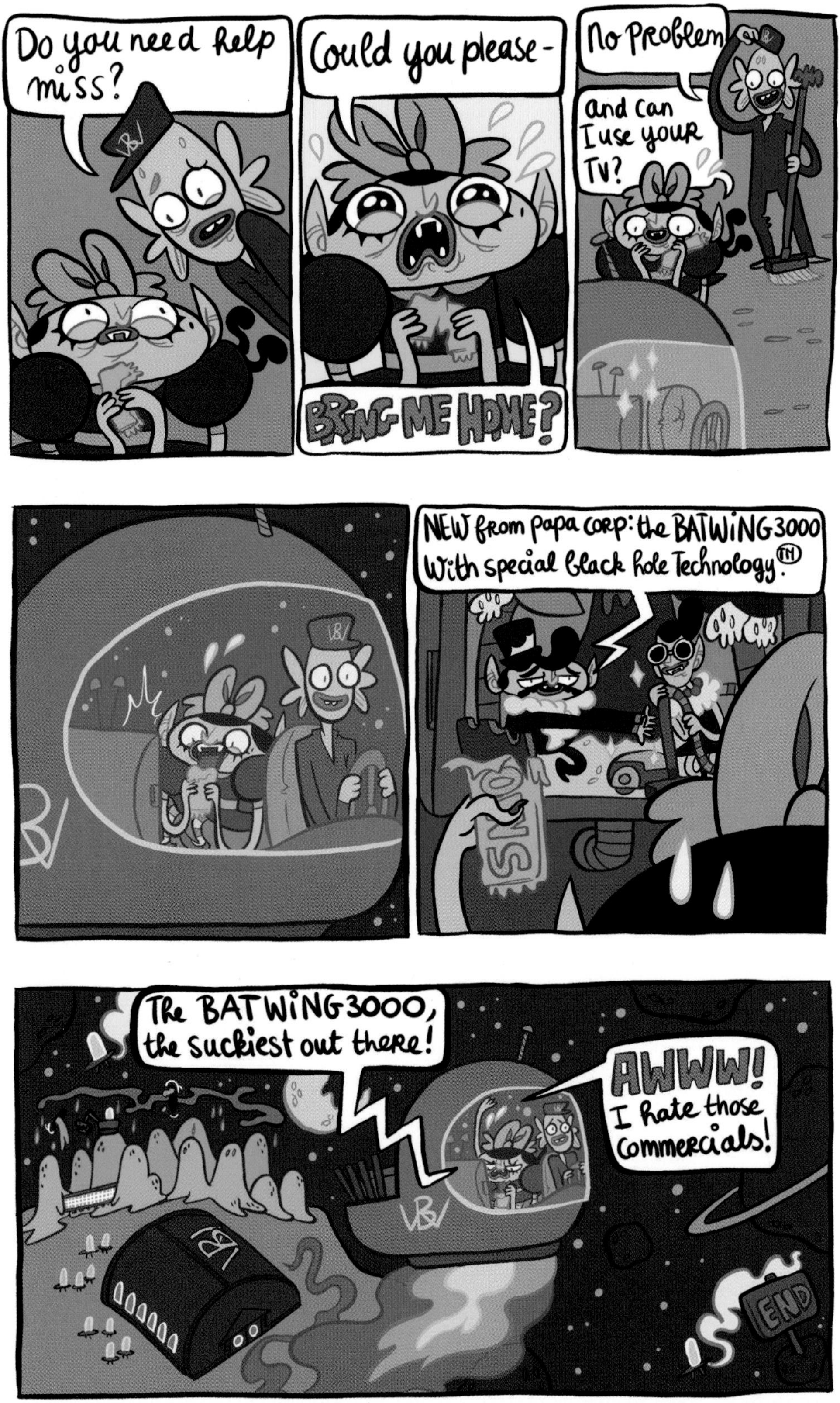
Do you need help miss?
Could you please-
BRING ME HOME?
No Problem
and can I use your TV?
NEW from papa corp: the BATWING3000 With special black hole Technology(TM).
The BATWING3000, the suckiest out there!
AWWW! I hate those commercials!
END

NO FACE

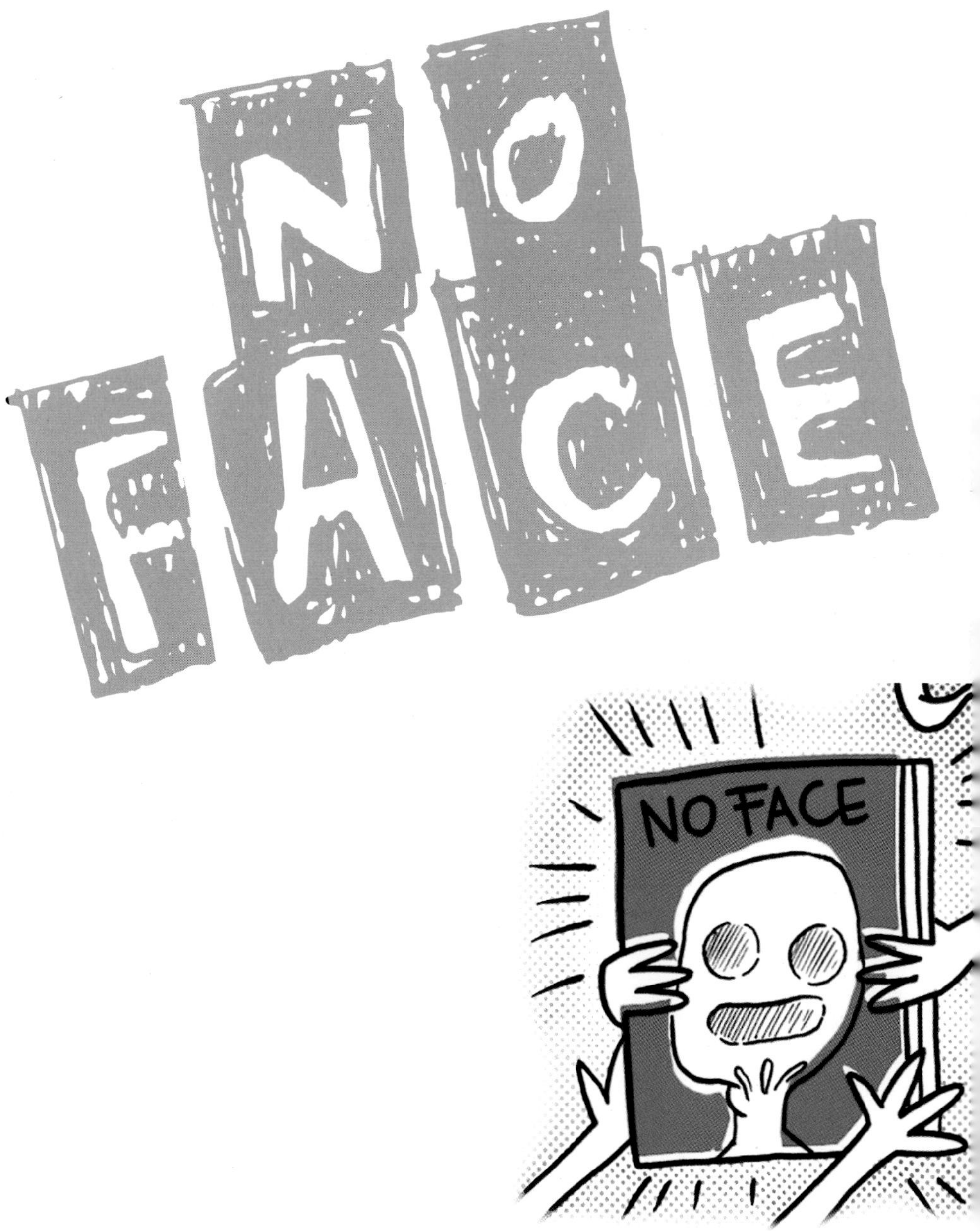
NO FACE

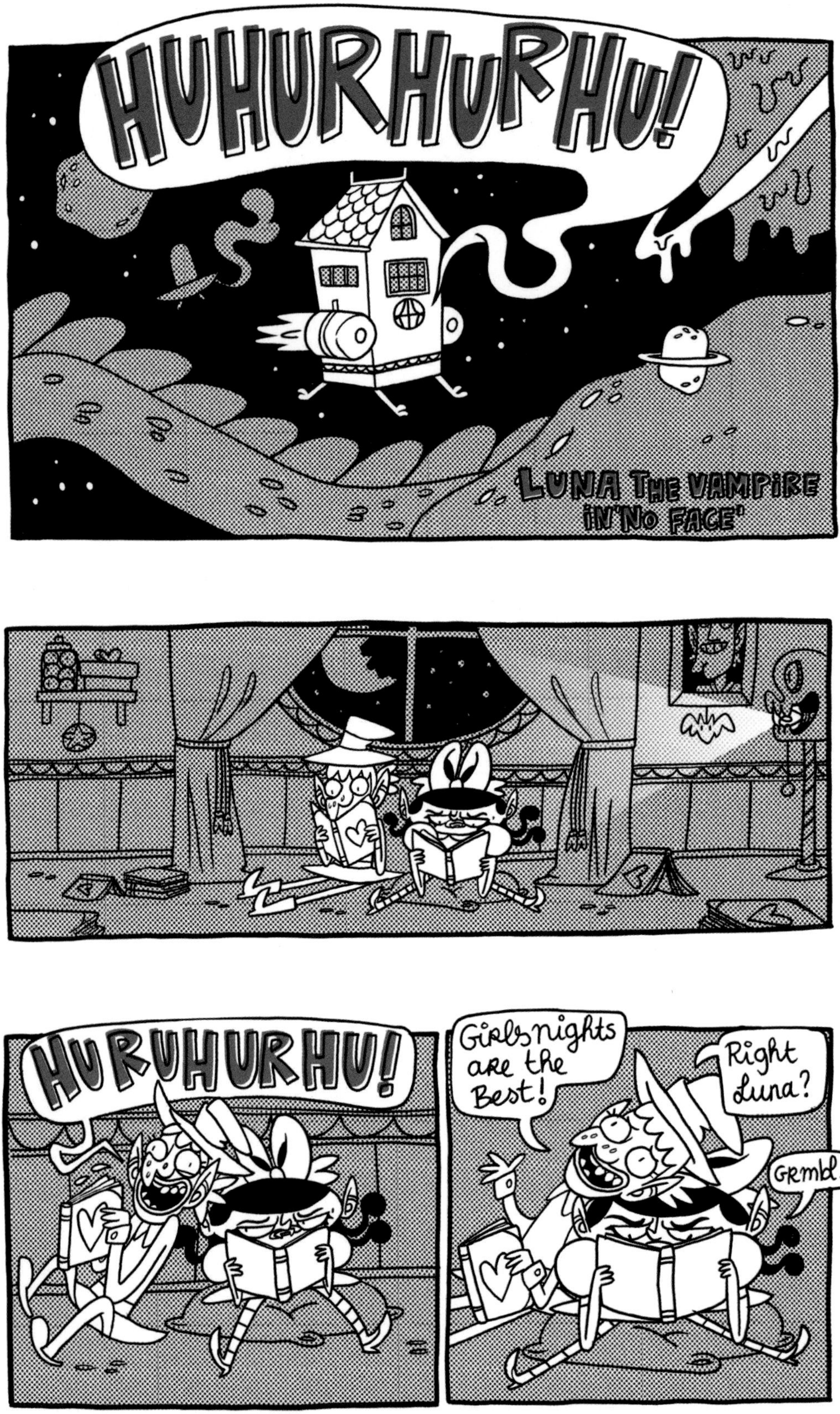
HUHURHURHU!
LUNA THE VAMPIRE
IN 'NO FACE'
HURUHURHU!
Girls nights are the Best!
Right Luna?
GRMBL...

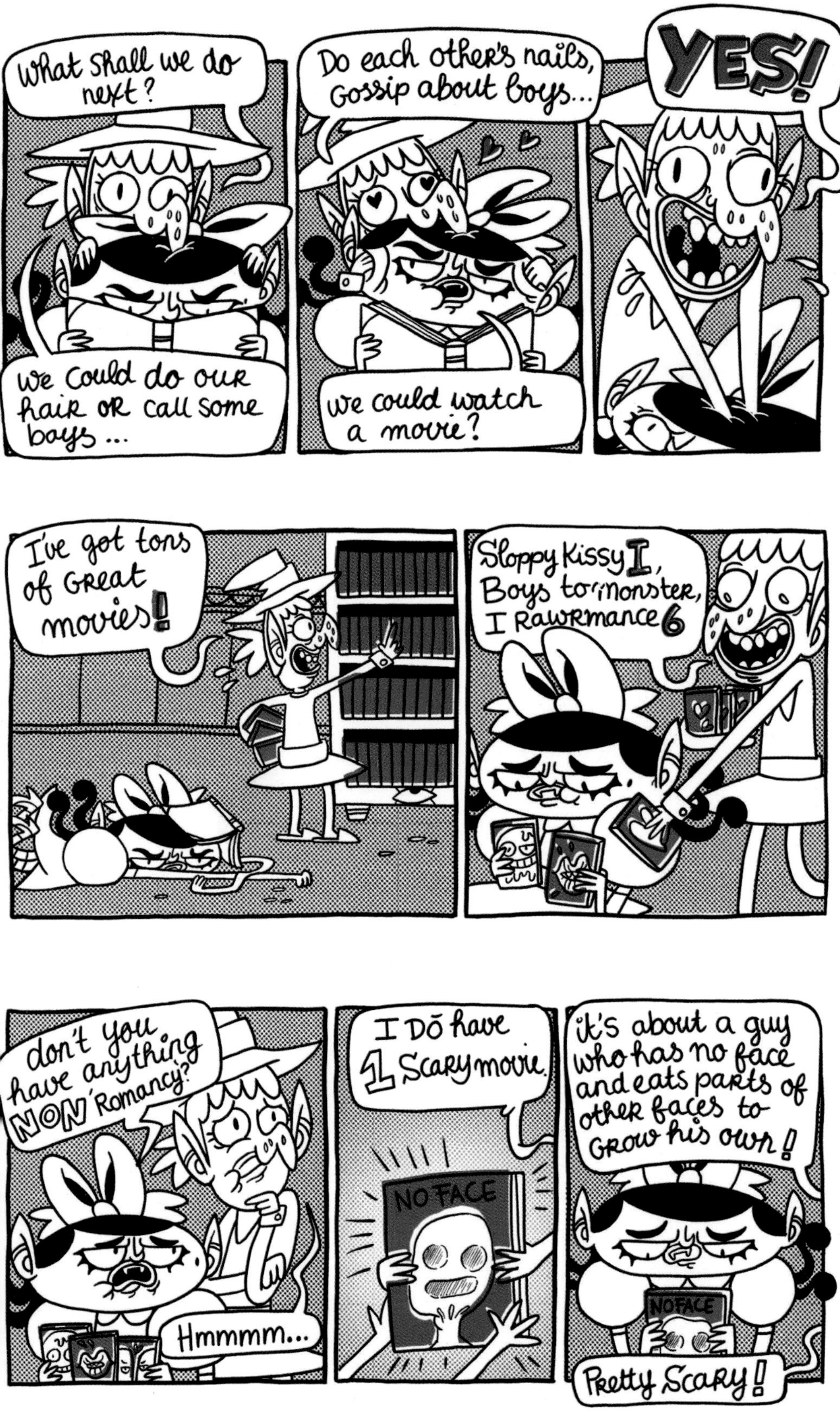
What shall we do next?
We could do our hair or call some boys...
Do each other's nails, Gossip about boys...
We could watch a movie?
YES!
I've got tons of Great movies!
Sloppy Kissy I, Boys to monster, I Rawrmance 6
don't you have anything NON Romancy?
Hmmmm...
I DO have 1 Scary movie.
NO FACE
it's about a guy who has no face and eats parts of other faces to Grow his own!
NOFACE
Pretty Scary!

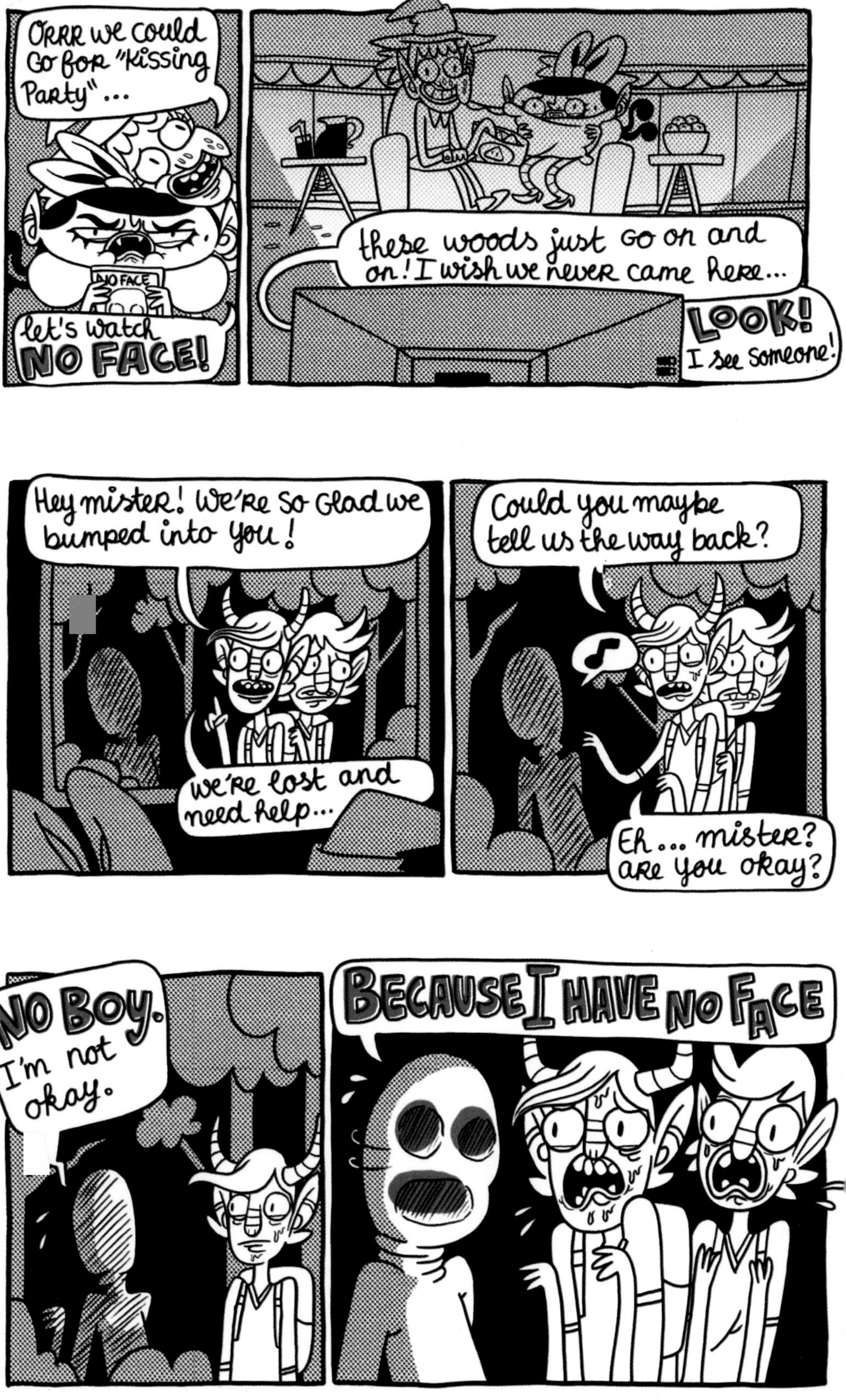
ORRR WE COULD GO FOR "KISSING PARTY"...
LET'S WATCH NO FACE!
NO FACE
THESE WOODS JUST GO ON AND ON! I WISH WE NEVER CAME HERE...
LOOK! I SEE SOMEONE!
HEY MISTER! WE'RE SO GLAD WE BUMPED INTO YOU!
WE'RE LOST AND NEED HELP...
COULD YOU MAYBE TELL US THE WAY BACK?
EH... MISTER? ARE YOU OKAY?
NO BOY. I'M NOT OKAY.
BECAUSE I HAVE NO FACE

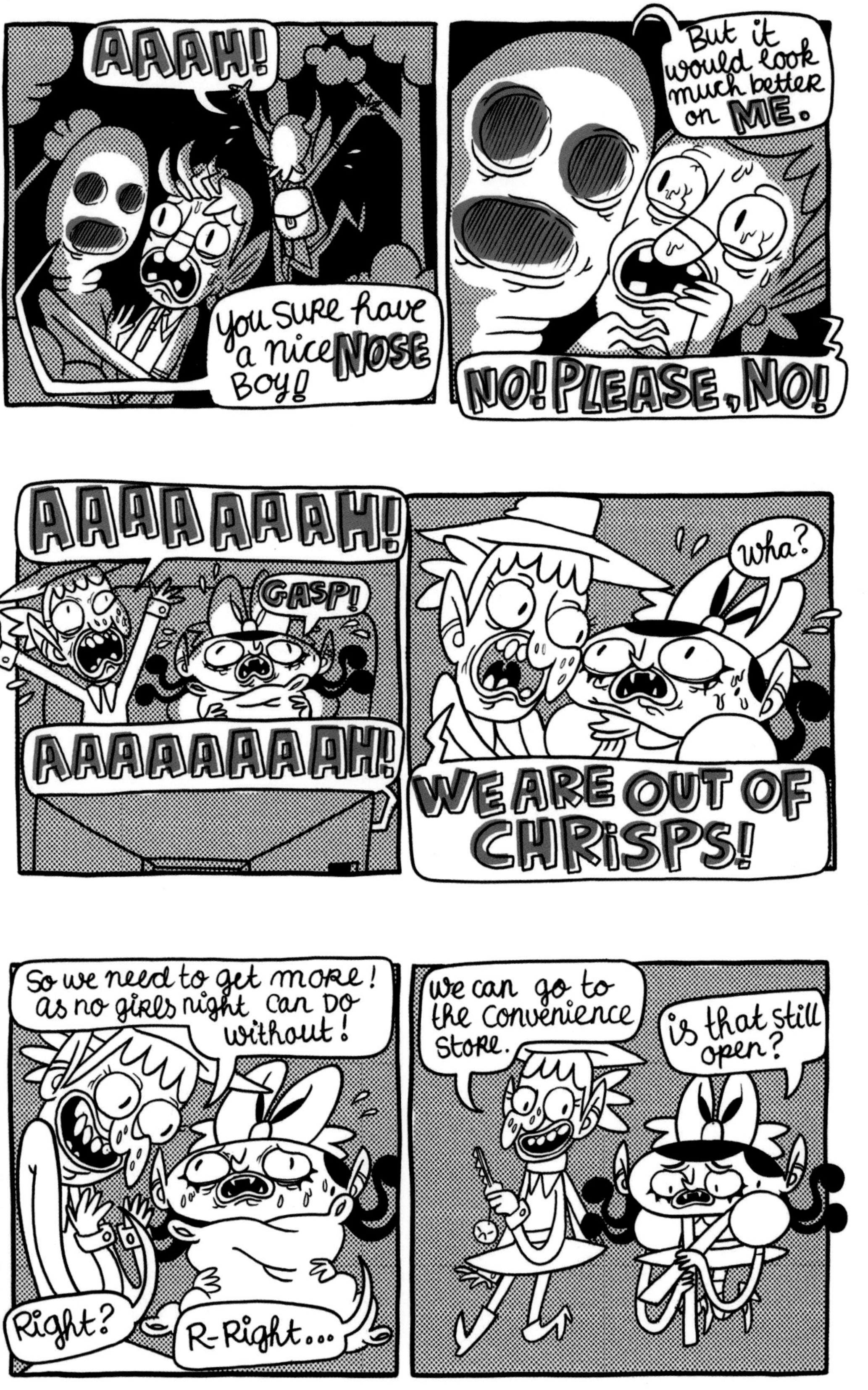
AAAH!
You sure have a nice NOSE boy!
But it would look much better on ME.
NO! PLEASE, NO!
AAAAAAAAH!
GASP!
AAAAAAAAAH!
Wha?
WE ARE OUT OF CHRISPS!
So we need to get more! as no girls night can do without!
Right?
R-Right...
We can go to the convenience store.
is that still open?

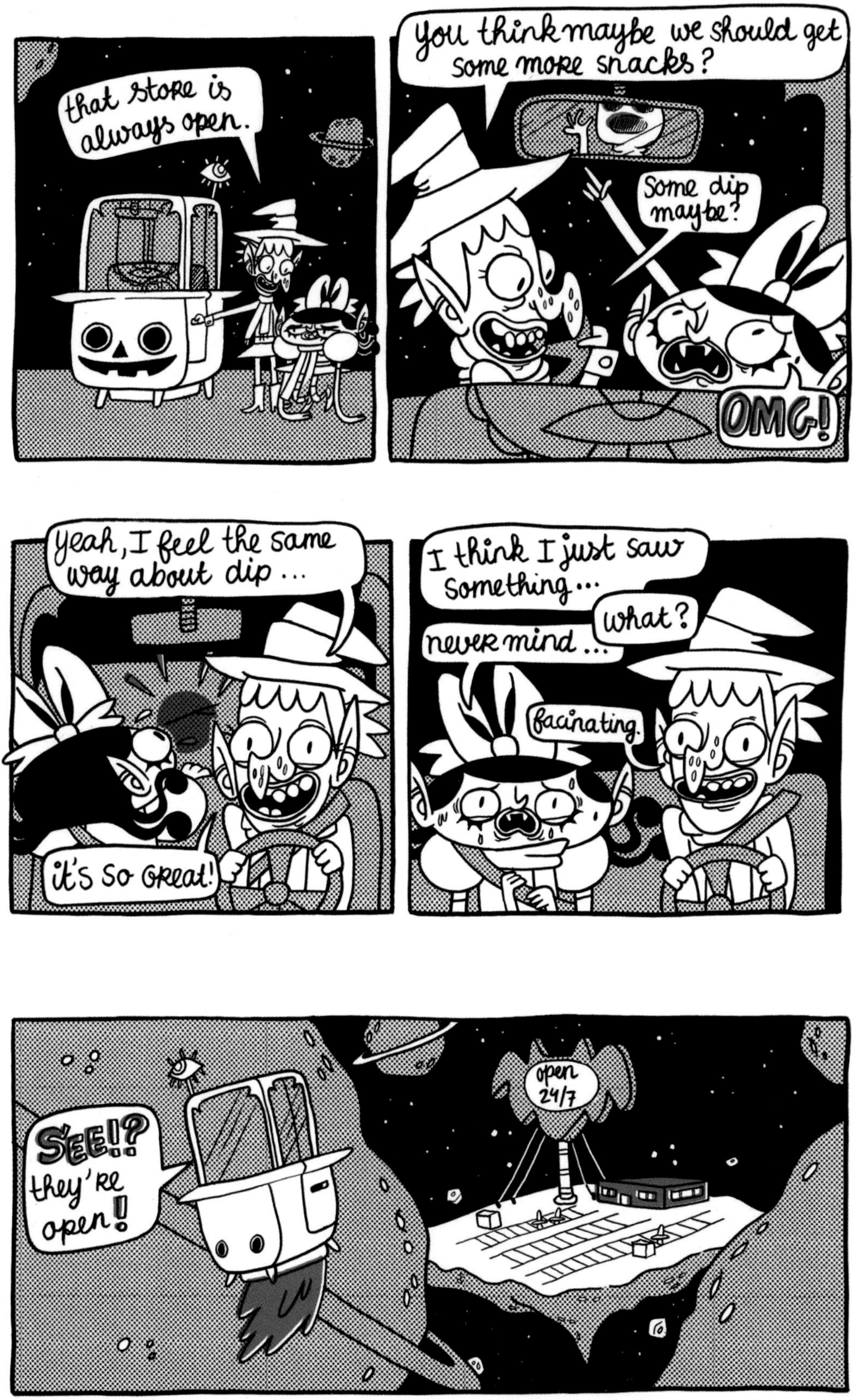
that store is always open.
You think maybe we should get some more snacks?
Some dip maybe?
OMG!
yeah, I feel the same way about dip...
it's so great!
I think I just saw something...
what?
never mind...
facinating.
open 24/7
SEE!? they're open!

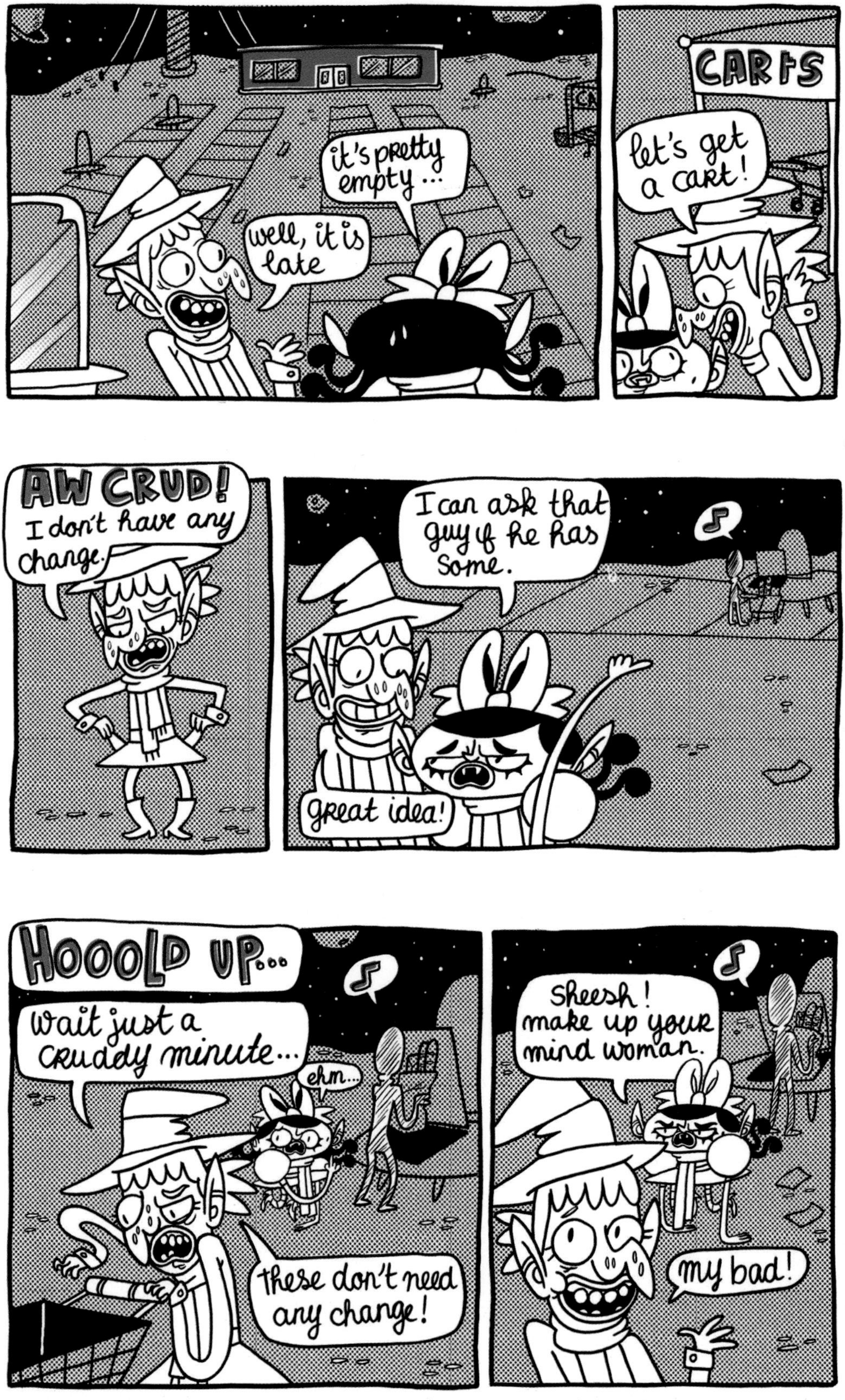
it's pretty empty...
well, it is late
CARTS
let's get a cart!
AW CRUD!
I don't have any change.
I can ask that guy if he has some.
great idea!
HOOOLD UP...
wait just a cruddy minute...
ehm...
these don't need any change!
Sheesh! make up your mind woman.
my bad!

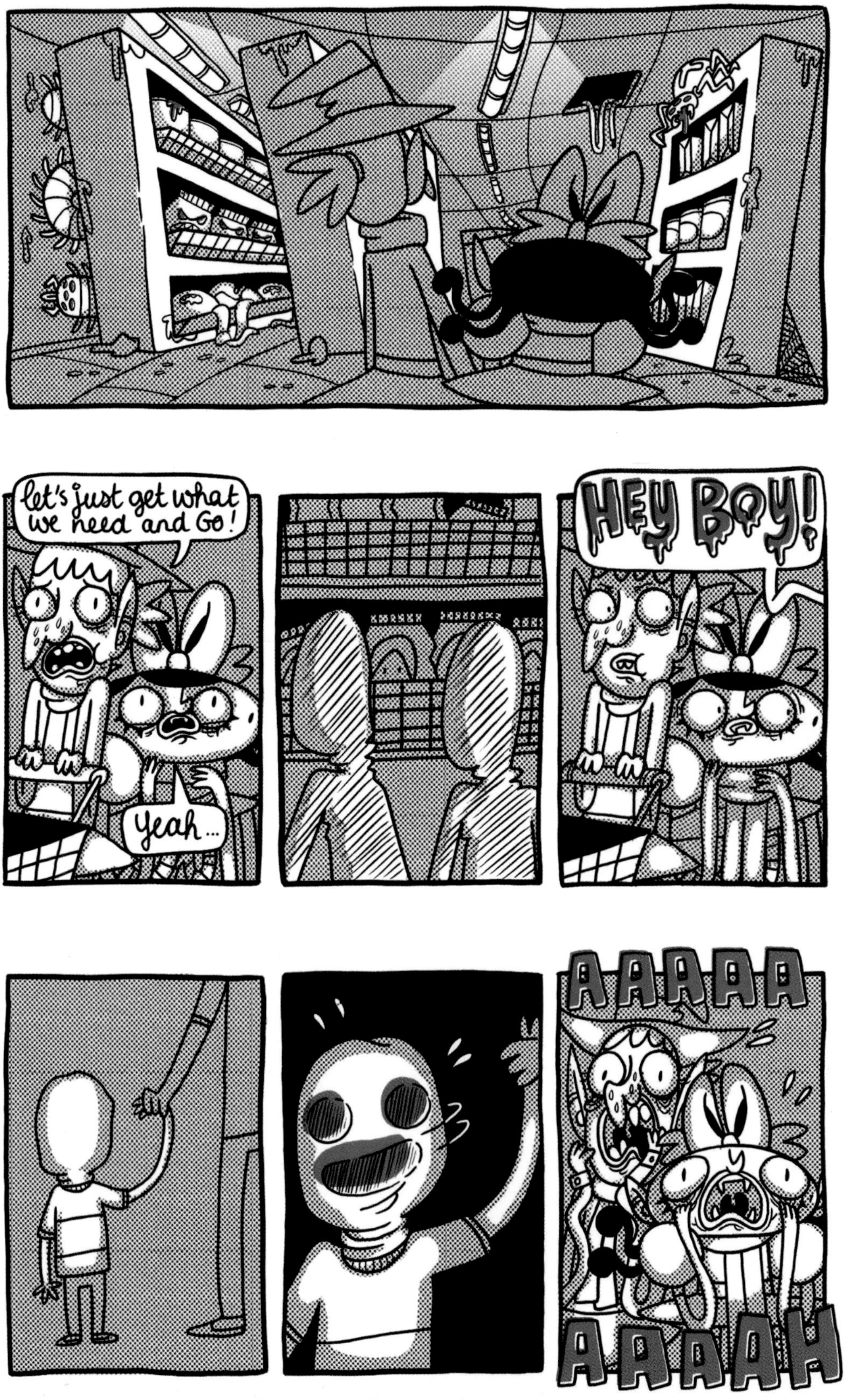
let's just get what we need and Go!
Yeah...
HEY BOY!
AAAAA
AAAAH

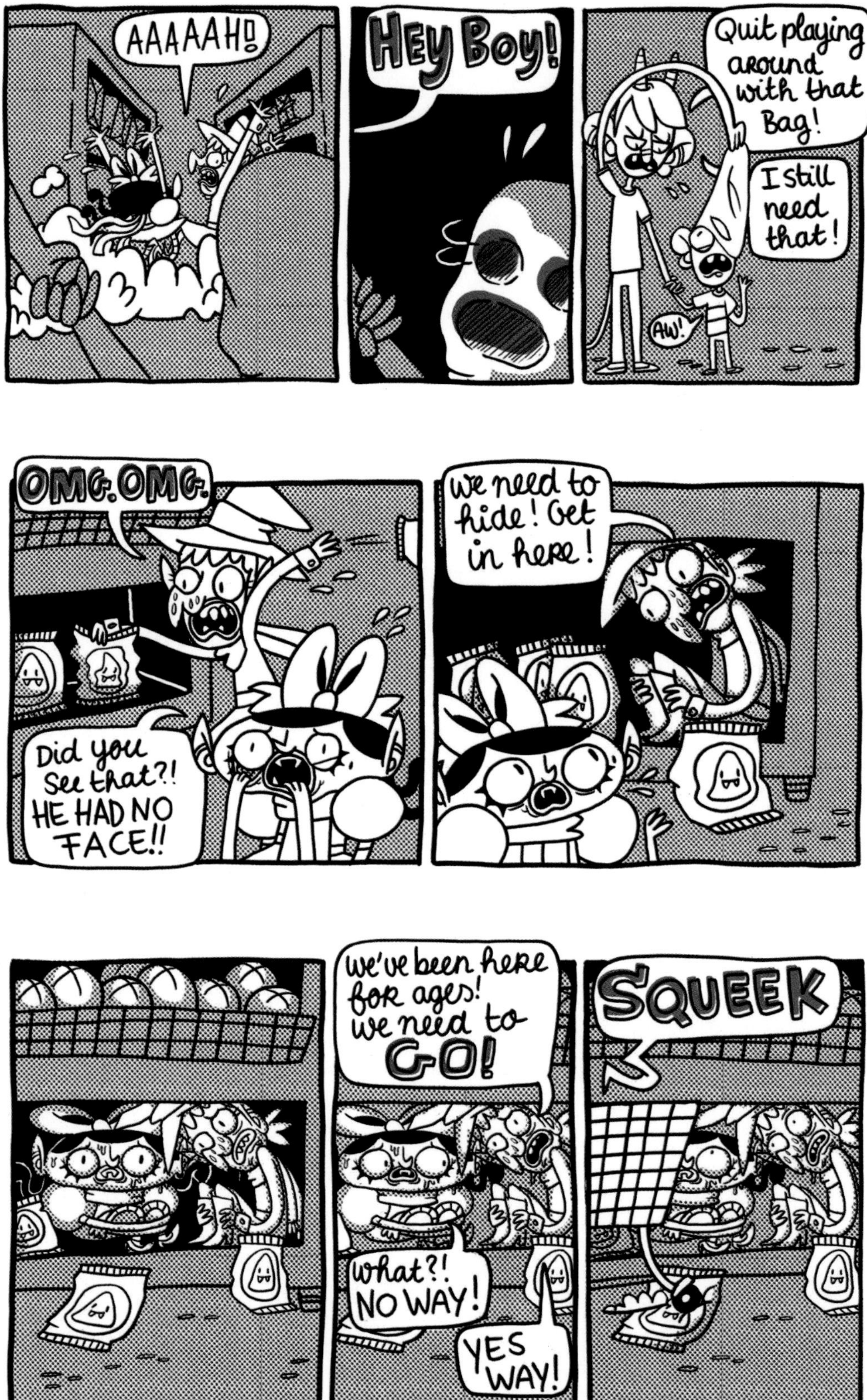
AAAAAH!
HEY BOY!
Quit playing around with that Bag!
I still need that!
AW!
OMG.OMG.
Did you See that?! HE HAD NO FACE!!
We need to hide! Get in here!
We've been here for ages! We need to GO!
What?! NO WAY!
YES WAY!
SQUEEK

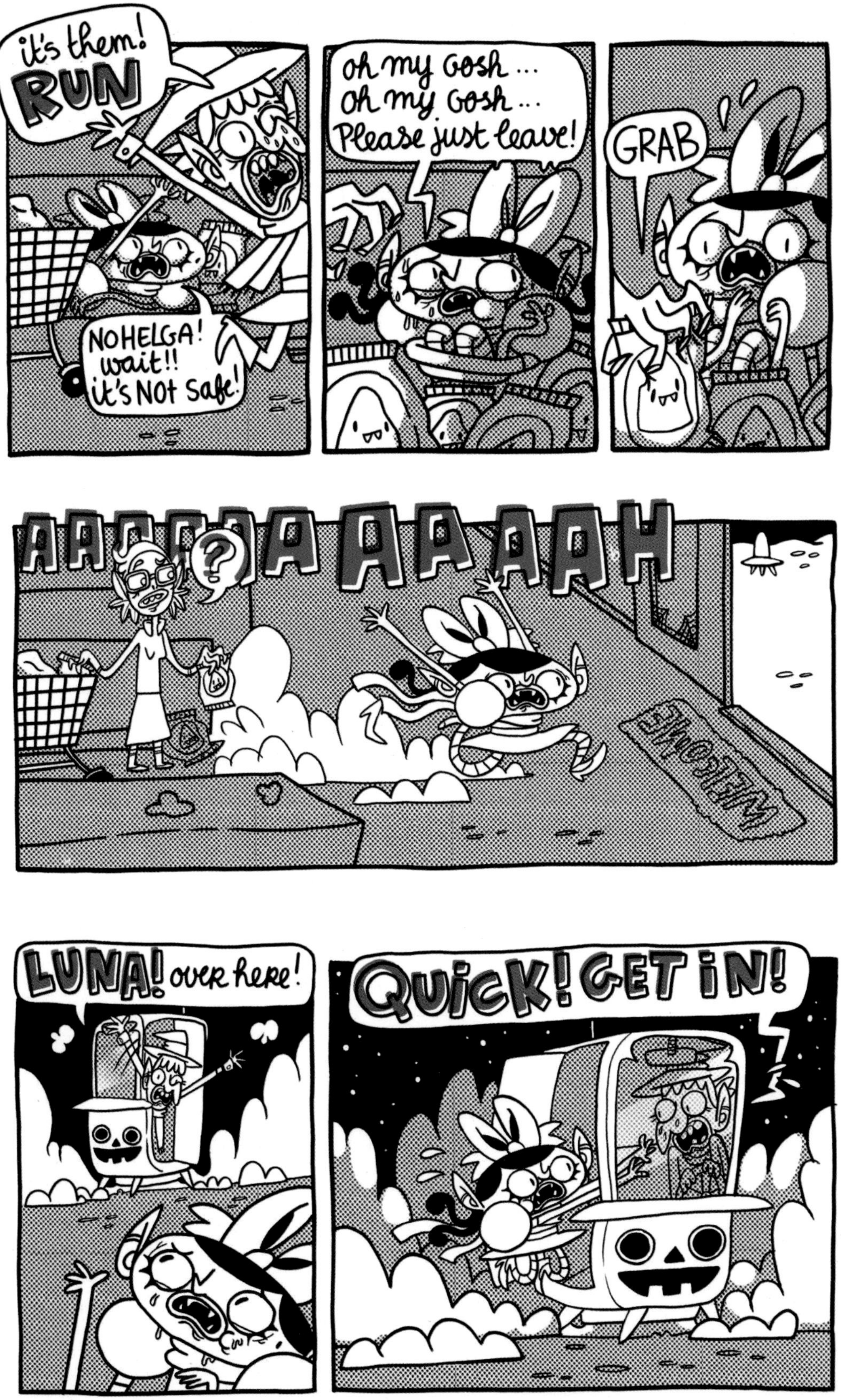
it's them!
RUN
NO HELGA! wait!! it's NOT safe!
oh my Gosh... oh my Gosh... Please just leave!
GRAB
AAAAAAAAAAH
?
WELCOME
LUNA! over here!
QUICK! GET IN!

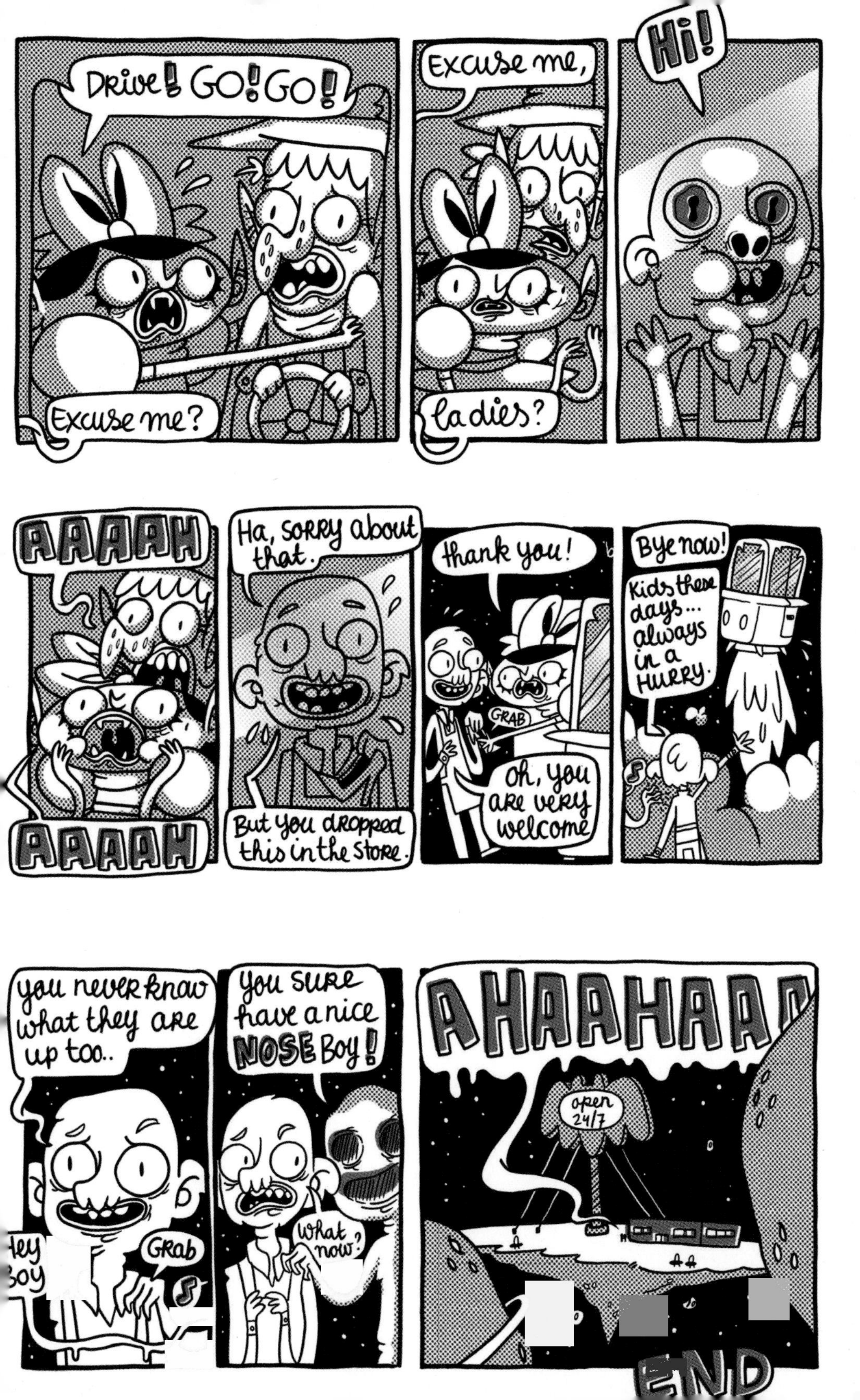

DRIVE! GO! GO!
Excuse me?
Excuse me,
ladies?
Hi!
AAAAH
AAAAH
Ha, SORRY about that.
But you dropped this in the store.
thank you!
GRAB
Oh, you are very welcome
Bye now!
Kids these days... always in a HURRY.
you never know what they are up too..
Hey Boy
GRab
You SURE have a nice NOSE Boy!
What now?
AHAAHAA
open 24/7
END

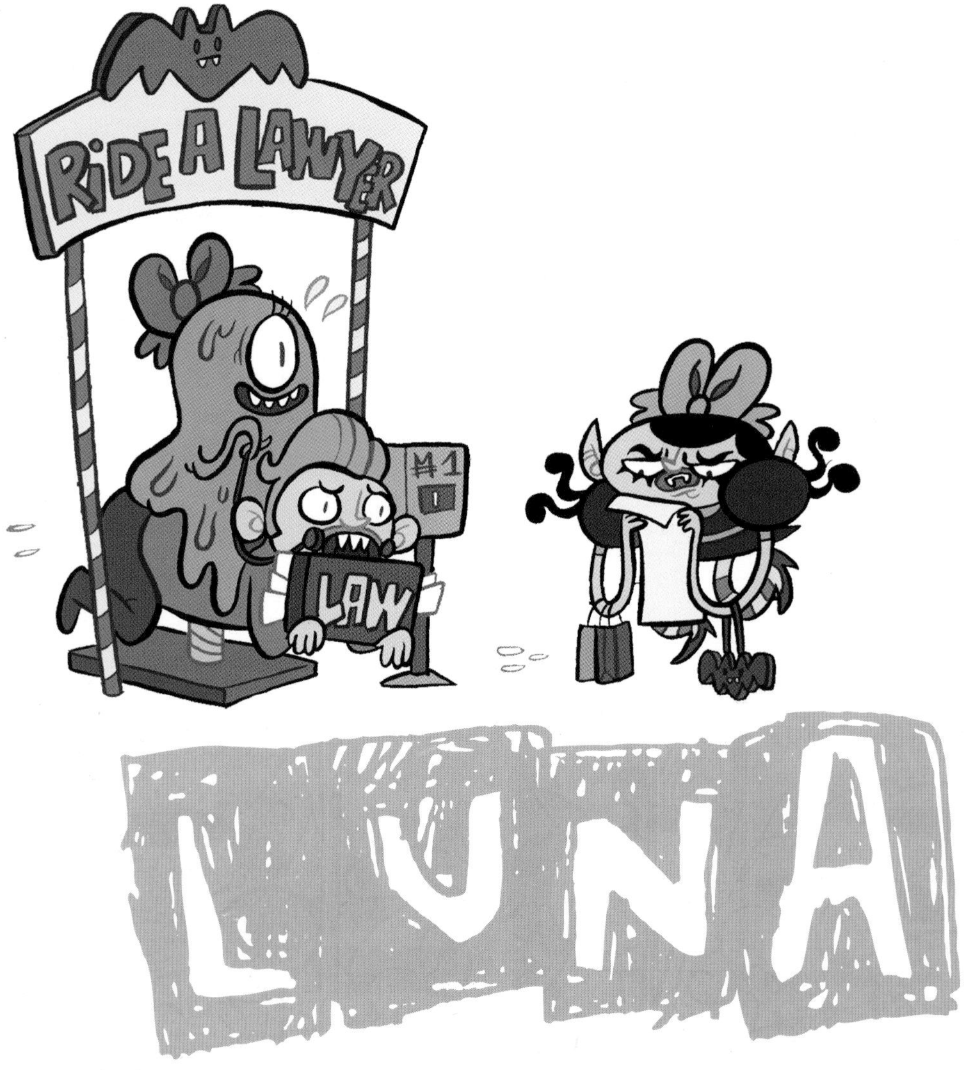
RIDE A LAWYER
LAW

LUNA

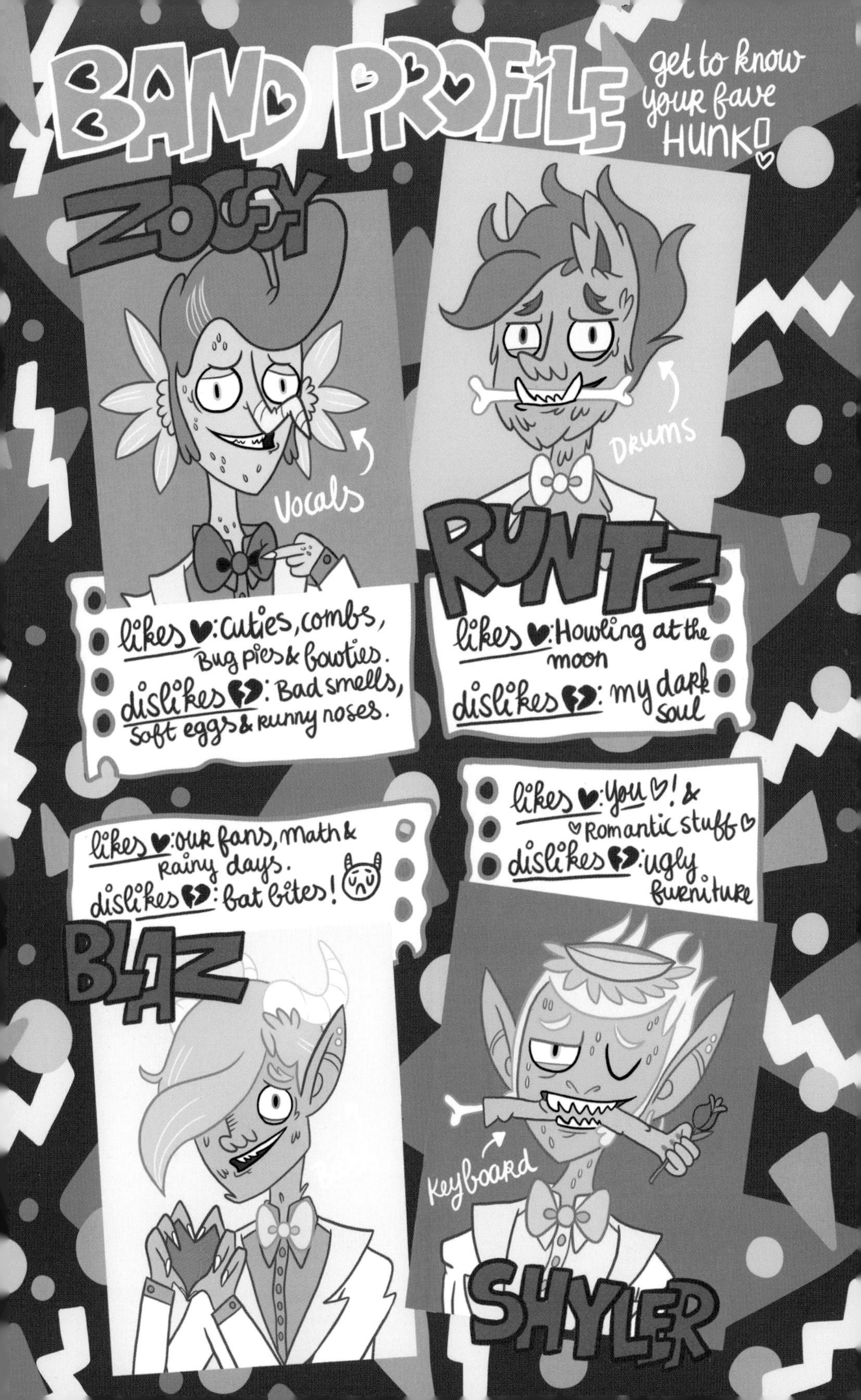
BAND PROFILE
get to know your fave HUNK!
ZOGGY
Vocals
likes: cuties, combs, Bug pies & bowties.
dislikes: Bad smells, soft eggs & runny noses.
DRUMS
RUNTZ
likes: Howling at the moon
dislikes: my dark soul
likes: our fans, math & rainy days.
dislikes: bat bites!
BLAZ
likes: You! & Romantic stuff
dislikes: ugly furniture
Keyboard
SHYLER

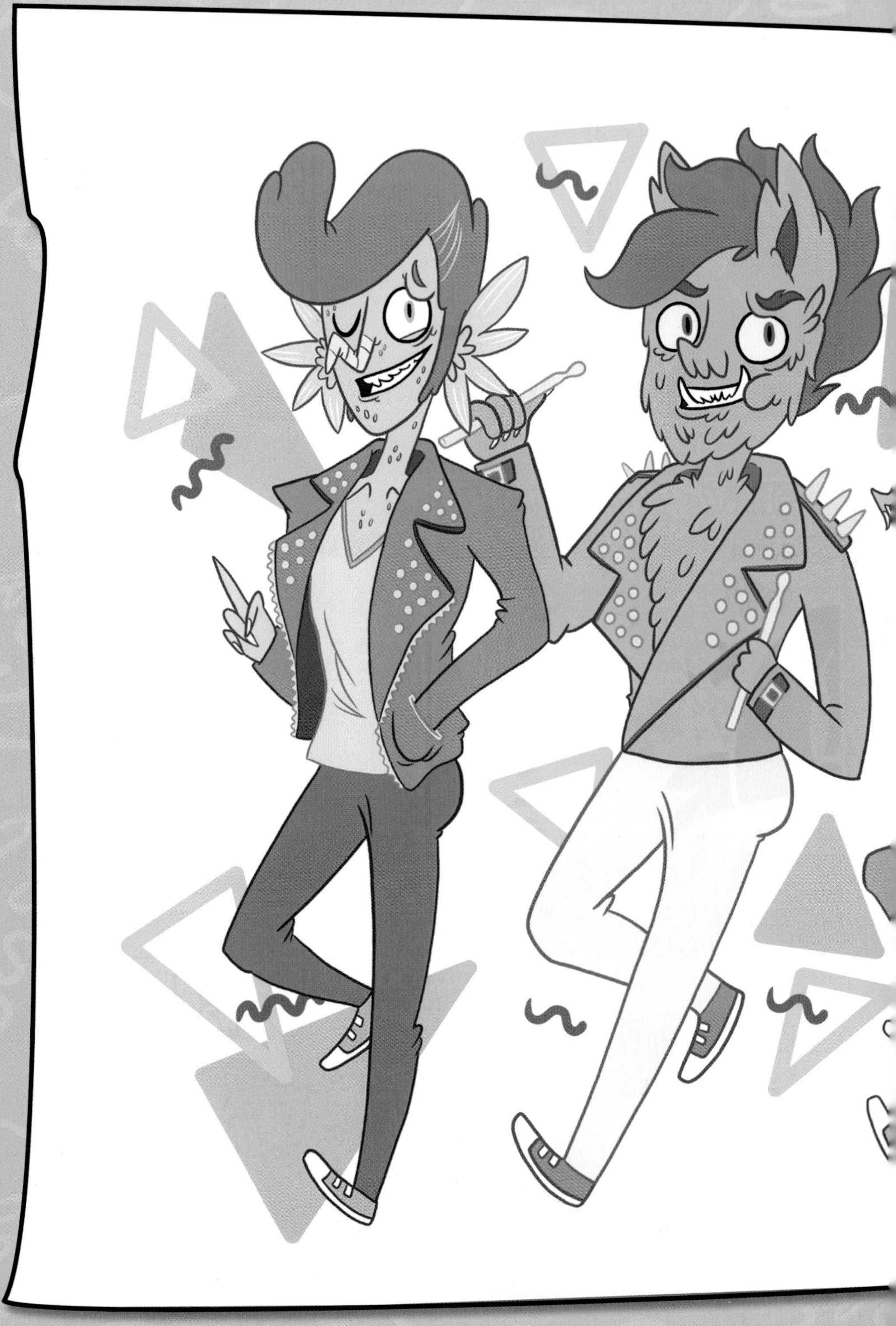

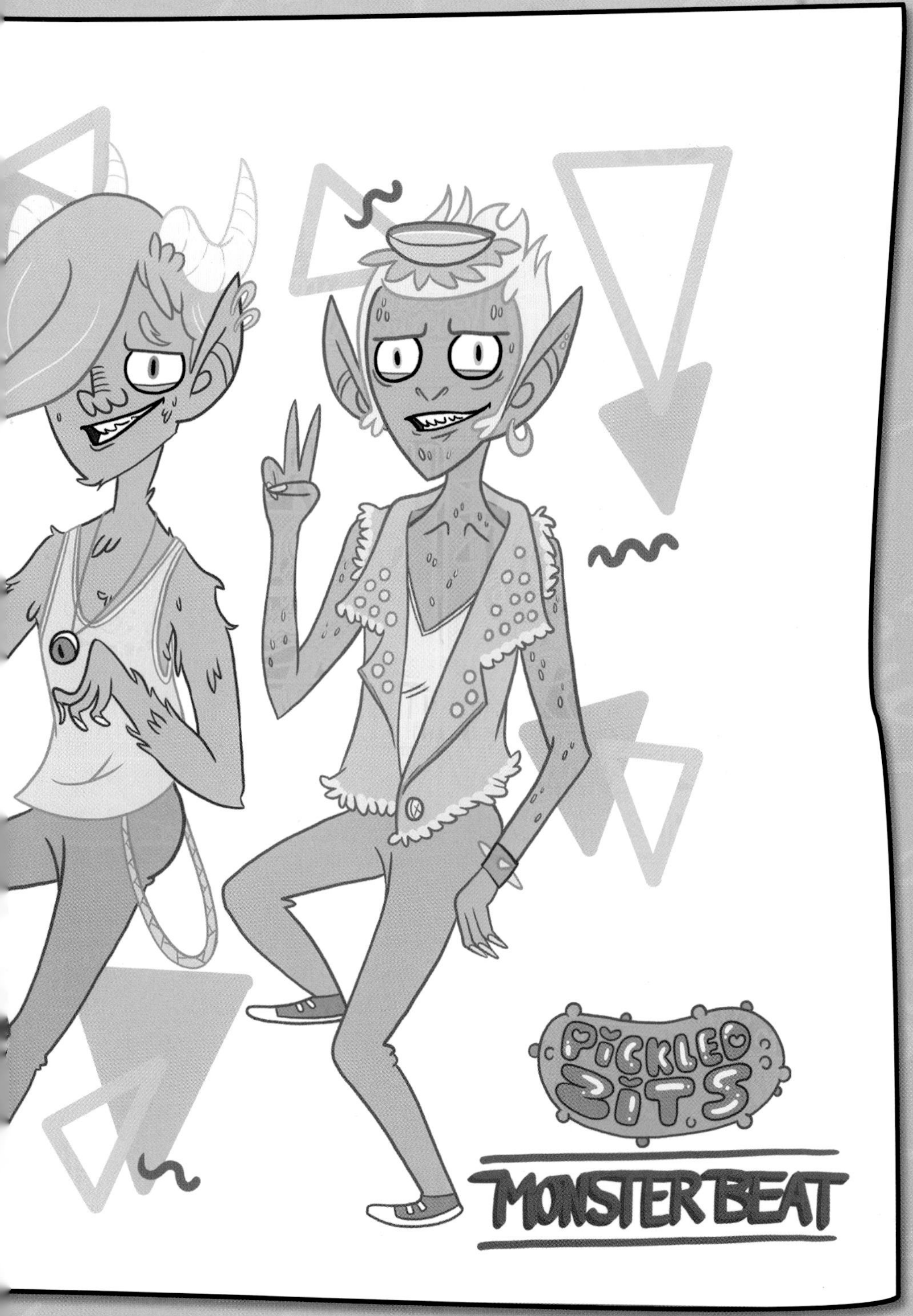
PICKLED BITS
MONSTER BEAT

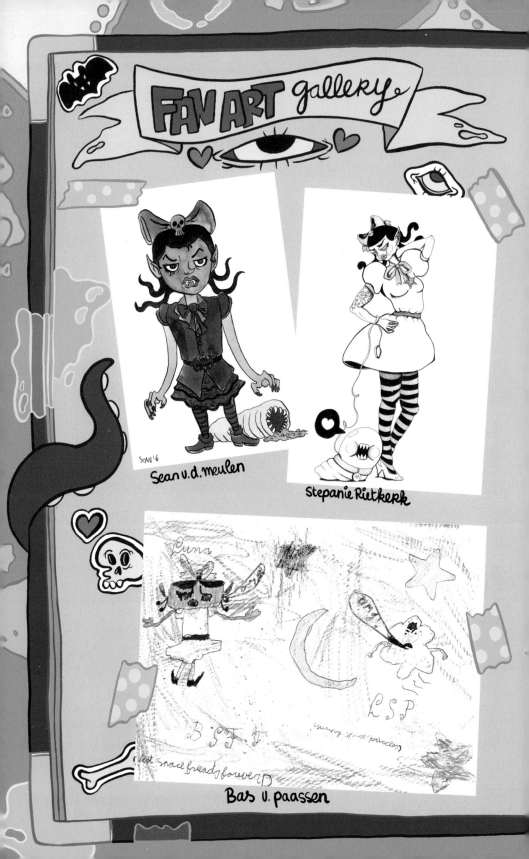

FAN ART gallery

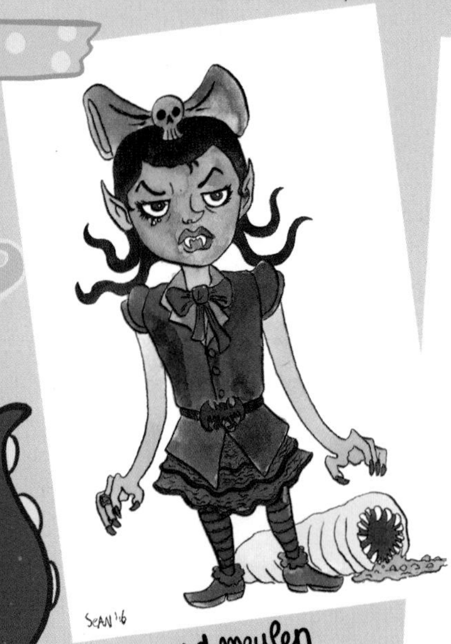

SEAN '16

Sean v.d. meulen

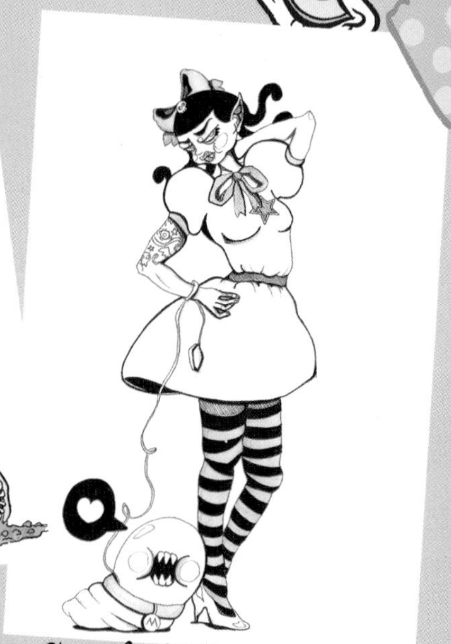

Stepanie Rietkerk

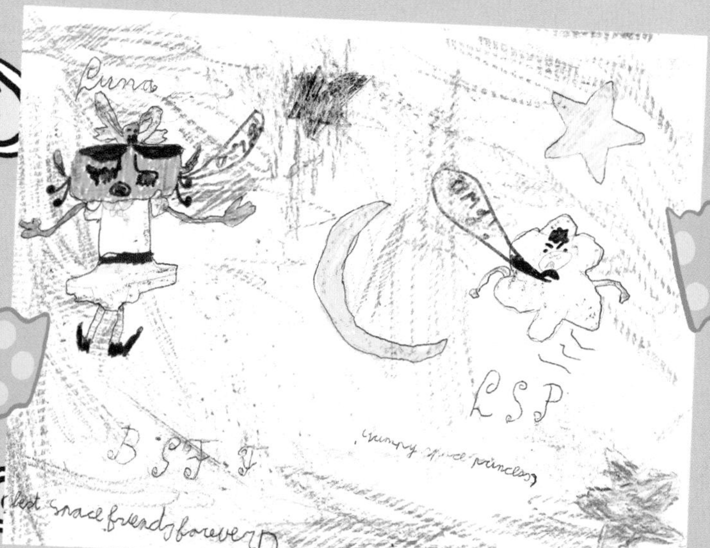

Luna
OMG
LSP
lumpy space princess
B.S.F.F.
best snace friends forever

Bas v. paassen

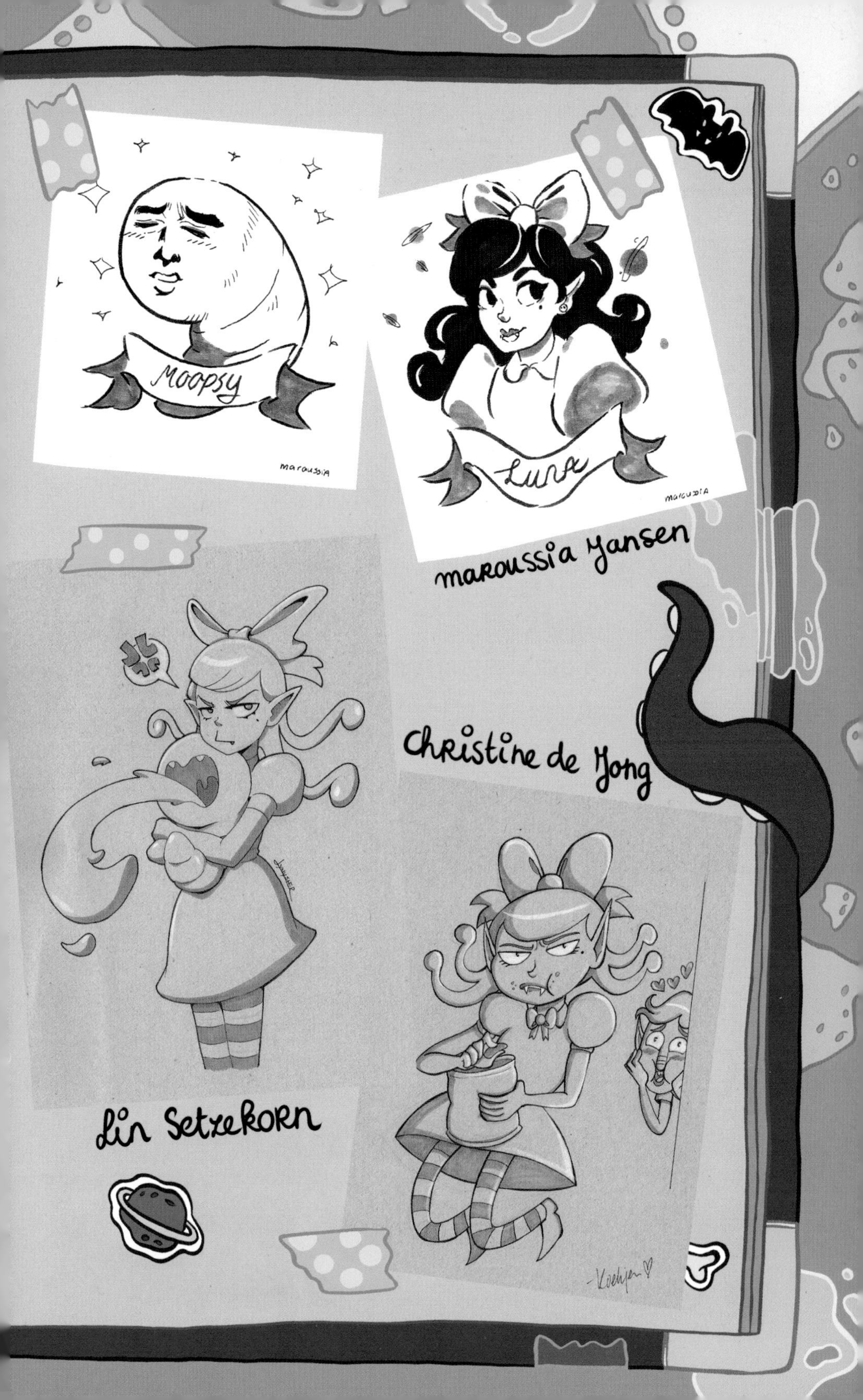
Moopsy
maroussia
Luna
maroussia
maroussia Jansen
Christine de Jong
Lin Setzekorn

Yasmin Sheikh has been a freelance artist for more than 15 years. Her clients include Lego, *Playstation Magazine*, Sony, Fundemic Games, Abstraction Games, and DoubleDutch Games, among others. When not producing commissioned work, she focuses on her comic, *Luna the Vampire*, which is published by IDW. She lives in the Netherlands.

Twitter: @nerderella
Instagram: instagram.com/nerderella
Website: www.nerderella.com

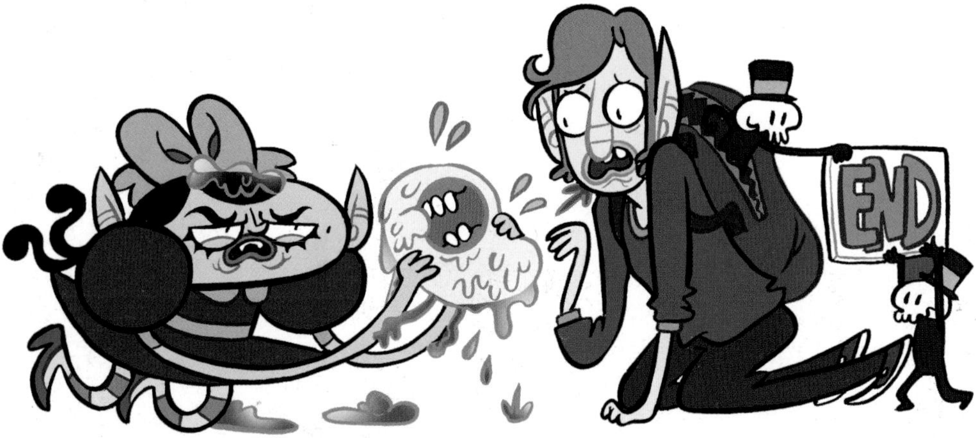
END